10/10

D1572205

# The Fight for San Bernardo

# THE FIGHT FOR SAN BERNARDO

## JACK CURTIS

THORNDIKE
CHIVERS

This Large Print edition is published by Thorndike Press, Waterville, Maine, USA and by BBC Audiobooks Ltd, Bath, England.

Thorndike Press, a part of Gale, Cengage Learning.

The text of this Large Print edition is unabridged.

Other aspects of the book may vary from the original edition.

Set in 16 pt. Plantin.

---

**LIBRARY OF CONGRESS CATALOGING-IN-PUBLICATION DATA**

Curtis, Jack, 1922–
   The fight for San Bernardo / by Jack Curtis.
      p. cm. — (Thorndike Press large print Western)
     ISBN-13: 978-1-4104-2613-0 (large print : hardcover)
     ISBN-10: 1-4104-2613-0 (large print : hardcover)
     1. Large type books. I. Title.
   PS3505.U866F54 2010
   813'.54—dc22                 2010008038

---

BRITISH LIBRARY CATALOGUING-IN-PUBLICATION DATA AVAILABLE

Published in 2010 in the U.S. by arrangement with Golden West Literary Agency

Published in 2010 in the U.K. by arrangement with Golden West Literary Agency.

U.K. Hardcover: 978 1 408 49150 8 (Chivers Large Print)
U.K. Softcover: 978 1 408 49151 5 (Camden Large Print)

Printed in the United States of America
1 2 3 4 5 6 7 14 13 12 11 10

# THE FIGHT FOR SAN BERNARDO

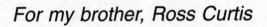

*For my brother, Ross Curtis*

In everything that can be called art there is a quality of redemption. It may be pure tragedy, if it is high tragedy, and it may be pity and irony, and it may be the raucous laughter of the strong man. But down these mean streets a man must go who is not himself mean, who is neither tarnished nor afraid.

*The Simple Art of Murder,*
Raymond Chandler
(Vintage Books, a division of
Random House.)

# 1

The redhead was an artist, his canvas the tan, sweat-damp rump of a two-year-old bull, his brush an iron rod curved and flattened at the end and heated to a cherry red, his subject the Hat brand that he was creating freehand from a Lazy L.

The bull's head was stretched out on the sandy ground by a lass rope held taut by a slim yellow-haired kid forking a ribby pinto. Another youngster knelt by the piggin' string hobbles he'd whipped around the fallen bull's hocks.

I didn't know any of them except from their work.

The redhead stuck his tongue out of the corner of his mouth and frowned as he concentrated on making his fourth masterpiece of the day.

They'd pushed about twenty head into a dry box canyon way off to hell and gone in the middle of Texas and meant to rebrand them all.

Maybe a quarter of the bunch were unbranded mavericks they might have had free for the taking, but it wasn't their way. They wanted everything with four legs and horns.

Thin and wiry as Apaches, they were raggedy-assed, underfed kids that had grown up in the cactus and mesquite land until the artist discovered he had a God-given talent with a running iron and didn't want to short his potential.

Left to pursue his goal, he'd have created a substantial herd of Hat brand cows out of nothing much more than his time, talent, and imagination.

The trouble was, every time the Hat brand increased, the Lazy L showed a decrease, and my job was to see everybody followed the rules.

I didn't know, but I could guess they came off a scratch-dirt ranch somewhere within about thirty miles. Likely Pa was dead and Ma didn't give a damn, and if the three weren't brothers, they were cousins.

The land made a spiny, droughty home that gave nothing away free and made hair-trigger desperados out of its children.

They were so confident out in the big lonely they'd forgotten to have a place to run to in case a stock detective happened by.

It wasn't just a happening. I'd been closing on them for a week, and now I had the stopper to their bottle. They couldn't go over the canyon walls, and they couldn't go over my Winchester .44-40.

I knelt behind a broken ledge in the entrance of the box canyon with the saddle gun cradled in my hands and hoped they'd be sensible.

Then I thought if these razor-backed, cactus-bred, mesquite-whipped kids were at all sensible, they'd do every damned thing possible to stay out of the Huntsville Pen.

At that moment I knew how it would probably go, but thinking that way was not going to help any.

What are you waiting for, Sam? Start the *pachanga.*

Standing in the clear, I pointed the carbine their way and yelled, "Drop your guns!"

It took them a couple of long seconds to figure out there was another human being on the earth, then another second or two to understand that he wasn't a friend.

"Drop the damn guns!" I yelled again, moving closer.

The redhead, instead of unbuckling his gunbelt, raised his hands shoulder high with the running iron gripped in his right fist. "Who are ya?"

His voice was high and thin as a yucca thorn in the still canyon air.

"Sam Benbow. Stockmen's Association. Now drop them damn guns!"

The one on the horse worried me most. I'd have rather he was on the ground where I could see his hands.

"What're you aimin' to do?" the redhead yelled back.

"I'm aimin' to take you into Lampasas for trial," I said, moving at them a step at a time, the carbine cocked and ready.

"Us'ns?" The redhead laughed thinly. "Go all that way for burnin' a bull's hide?"

"You're goin' one way or another," I came back at him. "Now drop the guns before I cut loose my wolf!"

"That ain't no wolf," Redhead crowed. "That's a polecat!"

Stopping within handgun range, I said, "Boys, don't get any contrary ideas. I don't like this much more'n you do. Use your left hands and unbuckle your gun belts."

"Sure now, old timer," the redhead said, glancing quick at the boy on the pinto. "We're plumb peaceable, but you kind of come at a bad time for us."

"I'll kill you deader'n hell, you don't mind

right now," I said, plain as I could.

"I don't reckon so" — the redhead let a little smile slash across his thin lips — "or you'da already done it. . . ."

Here it comes. Make your play.

"You're lookin' kind of tuckered out and weary-boned," the redhead drawled. "Better you just go back and tell them stockmen there ain't nothin' out here but a few tick-bit mavericks."

I had my first two moves in my head already, but he wasn't waiting.

"Here! Catch this, old timer." He smiled, threw the running iron at me, and stabbed his hand down to the old hogleg on his hip.

Now you do a dance you know well enough after learning a few swing-your-partner steps in the past twenty years or so, I thought. You pivot on your right foot, bringing your left leg around so the iron flies on by, and you've got the stock on the carbine extended as you continue the turn, catching the redhead smack across his cheekbone, and, following through with a graceful do-si-do, you're kicking the yellow hair in the knee and coming back with the carbine stock like you were paddling a canoe, and you catch him on the jaw as he falls. Then you're at the promenade you haven't planned.

Depends on what the boy on the pinto does. He can't run.

I was hoping he'd quit, but he sank his spurs and drove the pinto at me.

I lost the carbine grabbing the pinto around the neck to keep from being stomped. He clipped my left arm with a front hoof, and I fell under him, and he stepped on my chest as he went over. I drew my Peacemaker, rolling to my left.

The kid on the pinto aimed a rusty old Colt in my direction and fired, but the pinto was giving him too rough a seat for him to be accurate. I sent a bullet buzzing by the pinto's ear that set him to bucking.

While I was trying to line up the rider a shot came from back by the branding fire, and I saw the redhead on one knee, the Colt in his shaking hand coming down for another when I quick-fired.

Dust punched out of his ragged flannel shirt.

The yellow-haired kid was up by now and firing wildly. Maybe he'd shot a coiled rattler or a few bottles off a fence post, but he'd never fought under pressure, and I did my best to put a ball through his gun hand.

It wasn't an easy shot the way he was moving, but his revolver jumped from the bloody hand, and I saw him fall away.

Hearing the pinto coming at a run, I rolled and glimpsed the young rider leaning over, sighting down his Colt's barrel.

My shot caught him under the ribs and lifted him clear of the saddle for a moment before he slumped over the crazed pinto's neck.

He held on for another fifty yards before slipping loosely off into the dirt.

I looked back at the redhead. Motionless. The yellow-haired one was flopped flat on his back.

I reloaded and slowly got to my feet, breathing hard and quick, an unwanted tremble in my hands.

"Damn, damn, damn . . ." I was talking out loud, trying to get the pressure out of my chest. "Damn fools . . . oh . . . hell . . ."

It wasn't the redhead so much. He'd called the play, and he'd died quick. It wasn't the kid on the pinto so much either. He'd done his best to kill me, and I'd done what I had to do, but it was the yellow-haired one that rocked me.

I'd tried to spare him, but the damn bullet had ricocheted off his old horse pistol and gone up his wrist, ploughed along the ulna, riding up the humerus, nicking the axillary, tearing on to the collarbone, where it finally broke out, making a new tunnel for the charging blood.

I pressed his greasy hat hard against the bright, spurting fountain with both hands.

Why do we do these things, I wonder. To give a kid another second of life? What could he do with it?

Long yellow hair splayed out around the thin face of a boy who might be fifteen years old. He stared up at a cloud in the sky like he was trying to remember something.

I leaned over him, scarlet blood squirming through my fingers, but I couldn't speak.

"You old bastard," he gritted as the darkness closed down on him and matted his fierce blue eyes and stopped his empty, beating heart.

I washed my hands in every creek and pond and tank on my way back to Austin, but I couldn't get rid of that slickness nor the sweet fat blood smell.

Riding into Main Street, I aimed directly for Henry Ruggles's Royal Bathhouse.

Henry looked up at me from his rocking chair and said, "Sam, you're dirty inside and out. I ought to charge you double."

I wasn't in the mood for dumb jokes.

"Send somebody over to the mercantile. I want a whole new set of clothes," I growled at him, and I went on back into the bathroom, where the boiler was fired up. The full-sized copper tub was still some short for my scarred-up old hulk.

The water was as hot as I could stand, and I built up a carpet of suds as I used a stiff brush on my hands and under the nails, then everywhere I could reach, but it wasn't enough.

You old bastard!

I scrub-brushed my hands again.

I saw the boy's dust-brushed face, the angry eyes, the light leaving, and I felt a great unbidden sob commence somewhere in the pit of my stomach and build up inside my chest until there was no holding back.

As the first groan broke from my throat I grabbed up a towel and held it tight over my face.

Bawling with pent-up grief and anger, I thought I heard the door open and close, but when I looked there was no one there, and I let the sorrow and despair surge and drain itself out, much as the blood had spouted from the boy's wound.

You're finished, Sam. You've downed too many too long.

Thinking about the whole of it, I thought I was weeping as much for the loss of my own good years as for the boy's. They were almost the same thing. Youth and hope, life and love, all wasted in the mill of time.

Ever since I'd joined up with General Jackson I'd been killing people. Most of them I hadn't even known.

I'd lived forty or so years and had nothing to show for it except a good steel-dust horse and a Padget brothers saddle, a Colt six-shooter and a Winchester saddle gun, a set of Petnecky spurs, and a job that included killing kids.

What a hell of a business to be in!

I heard the door open, and I didn't need to look up when I heard the raucous screech of my sometime partner.

"Hellsafire! You're goin' to be scalded like a butchered hog you ain't careful!"

" 'Lo, Skofe," I said.

"Want me to throw in some cold?" he kept on. "You boil your pizzle, it's liable to shrivel up and fall off."

"No."

"No, what?" He came up close. "I'm tellin' you, I've known of cases where a man sat overlong in hot water and came out singing like a chickadee."

"Skofe," I said tiredly, meaning for him to quiet down.

"I'd offer to scrub your back if you didn't take me wrong," he cackled.

I looked at his frail old purplish face, his

stringy gray hair, his rheumy gray eyes, and wondered if he'd ever had the blue fantods.

"Use the brush," I said, leaning forward.

I felt the welcome itching of the brush between my shoulder blades, and he asked, "Catch 'em?"

"Uh-huh." I nodded.

"Bring 'em in?"

"Nuh-huh." I shook my head.

"I knew I should have gone along," he croaked.

"You was too busy buckin' the broom around the dance floor showin' everybody how you rode the strawberry roan to a standstill."

"That wasn't the way it was," he declared disgustedly, tossing the brush onto the bench. "I was just teachin' my dear Wagon Tongue Emmy how to sweep the floor."

"You sure spurred the straw out of the poor critter."

"Emmy?"

"The broom."

"Sam Benbow, you better start talkin' sense, or I'm goin' to send you back to the bakery," he blustered indignantly.

A banty rooster, the top of his gray head came about to my shirt pocket, and while I'm starting to thicken up in the midsection like a full-grown bull, I'm not carryin' all that much extra tallow, and I still out-weighed him about two to one.

He'd been a professor of divinity at the University of Virginia at the start of the war and had joined up as a chaplain.

A year of trying to serve the God of love and the Satan of battle tore him up so bad, he took up the gun and saber and quit givin' burial speeches over the mounds of dead boys.

We met at the second battle of Manassas under Jeb Stuart. Rev. Skofer Haavik was an old captain by then, and I was a young lieutenant.

When the war ended, Skofe, having lost his faith and professor's chair as well as his family home, had nowhere to go except west.

Being oversized and well trained in kill-ing, I had no trouble finding work as a law-man to tide us over until we found whatever we thought was worth working for.

Skofer, troubled by his forced flip-flop from academic theology to splitting un-known enemies with his saber, had taken up joyous skylarking in order to accom-modate his refusal to look at what had been done to him.

Like most humor, his blithe high jinks were just one step removed from horror.

Straddling and bucking out a broom on the dance floor of the Brindle Bull Saloon was only incidental. Somehow after Shiloh, where we were both hurt, he avoided the serious side of life like it was rat fever.

"Commander wants to see you," Skofe muttered grimly, as if daring me to break his scrawny neck. "Said you had no business takin' a bath first."

"You go tell that fat son of a bitch I quit."

"You can't quit."

"Why the hell not? I been chasin' rustlers and crooked cattle brokers for too long. We've got enough saved, surely."

"We did," Skofer said, trying to look canny.

"Skofe, if you lost our stake —"

"No, no, I just invested it. Believe me, Sam, it'll double itself in a month. But we're goin' to need a little somethin' to keep us afloat."

"Skofe, believe me," I said, seriously as I could, "I mean to quit this. I'm at the end of my rope. We've got to get back to California."

"I swear a month from now we'll be rich enough to do it," Skofe said. "Have you ever known me to be wrong?"

He stood up straight and opened his hands wide to show how affronted he was by my attitude.

"Skofe, I'm done," I said tiredly. "Bein' a stock detective sounds like all you do is go around, scratch your ass, and check brands, but it's some worse."

"Don't worry about it," he said. "I doubt if the commander even has an assignment outside of Austin."

"Where's the money?" I asked, resigned to bad news already.

"A friend of Wagon Tongue Emmy is goin' to bring in a load of leftover Union uniforms. She buys 'em cheap and sells 'em high."

"You don't suppose folks around here might have somethin' against wearin' a Union uniform?" I shook my head, trying to hold my temper.

It was my fault for letting him know where I kept our stake.

"They're just like brand new," he said, puzzled by my pessimism.

The Brindle Bull wasn't much different from any other frontier saloon except its chief ornament was the stuffed head and neck of a brindle bull with horns seven feet across apiece.

Legend had it that he'd killed a grizzly bear, a puma, a jaguar, and numerous cowboys before somebody ambushed him long-range with a buffalo rifle for sport.

He wasn't looking so good anymore because occasionally a puncher in deep drink might see him coming at full charge and draw and fire in self-defense.

Both eyes were shot out, and his muzzle was blown open enough for some joker to put in a cigar.

Other merrymakers had hung items of ladies' underwear from his wide horns, as well as an ancient tin powder horn, a braided rope said to have been made from the hair of squaws killed at the battle of Sand Creek, a big curved brass hearing trumpet, a toy bugle, a big skunk skin, a stuffed iguana, and a thorny-looking blowed-up puffer fish.

Otherwise it was a bar with tables and a raised dance floor where you could get acquainted with the sporters for the price of a drink and close to matrimony for a month's pay.

Leap Malone, a thickset man with a ginger-colored beard and a way of clearing his nose by holding one nostril shut with a forefinger and blowing hard, usually missing the beard, came to greet us, pawing at the plank bar with a gray rag.

He was called Leap because someone had

figured out that every leap year he bought the house a drink.

"Beer," I said.

"One?" Leap grinned.

"Emmy about?"

"Lit out yesterday." He shook his head. "Her replacement's due in tonight."

"Sam" — Skofe coughed hoarsely — "she'll be back. She give me her word."

"Make it two, Leap," I said. "Skofe's beginning to sound like a bullfrog in the desert."

"I'll make it up to you, Sam," Skofe said when Leap brought the beer. "Just as soon as my inheritance gets straightened out."

"Sure, Skofe." I nodded, already aware that his inheritance had come in Confederate currency and that there was never going to be any straightening out.

He finished his glass in one breath, exhaled comfortably, and looked up at me like man's best friend.

I put a dollar on the counter and said, "Enjoy yourself. I've got to report to the commander."

"Don't go off half-cocked, Sam," Skofe said, tapping the bar importantly with the silver dollar.

"I'm resignin' and goin' to California."

"You can't, Sam. We ain't even got getaway

26

money."

"I guess we can eat horny toads and rattlesnakes. It's better'n bad dreams."

The South Texas Cattlemen's Association office was located on Houston Avenue above the First Bank of Texas. It didn't amount to much more than a long, narrow room with a couple of rolltop desks, a big iron safe, and some hard wooden chairs.

The first desk was occupied by a sallow-faced young man wearing a black suit and string tie. On his desk was an open ledger, and in his hand was a steel-nibbed pen.

He looked up at me like I was a grub-liner lookin' for a handout and said, "Yes?"

Walking on by without speaking, I headed for the rear of the room, where the commander had his desk set at an angle so he had the best light over his bulky left shoulder.

The clerk sighed a faint protest and went back to his copying.

Broad and round, Commander Frazier looked up at me, and before he could speak I said, "I'm drawin' my time."

"What's the hurry?"

He put on a smile I didn't believe, rose to his full five and a half feet, shook my hand warmly, and gently guided me to a chair like I was his venerated grandfather.

"Have a cigar."

He extended the box. I passed.

Not only was he built like an outdoors Mexican oven, his head was a block with heavy convex features that were starting to droop down like hot candle wax. Offhand, you couldn't tell if he was a bulldog or a beardless Santa Claus, but I knew him well by now, and there was not a speck of gentleness, generosity, humor, or mercy in him. All bulldog he was.

"Hard trip?" he murmured, his deep-set eyes warm as a crocodile's.

"The three of 'em was changing Lazy Ls to Hats," I said. "They wouldn't come peaceable."

"Still — they were rustlers." The commander nodded, trying to sugar the pill.

"There wasn't a one over seventeen," I said. "I can't go no more of it."

"You've been working too hard, Sam." He nodded agreeably. "Suppose I offered you an easy excursion? Nothing to do except fish and hunt and play with the señoritas?"

Wondering what kind of a trap he was setting, I waited for more.

"There's nothing to it. The Volunteer Auxilliary Battalion of the Texas Rangers has everything under control. All you have to do is watch."

"No offense, but this is a little hard to figure."

"It's time I did you a favor, Sam," he said heavily, folding his big hands together. "Now things are starting to settle down."

"Seems like I heard that speech somewhere before," I murmured, eyeing him like he was a scorpion in my bedroll.

"Ever hear of a little town on out west called San Bernardo?" He smiled crosswise.

I nodded. "Near the border. Right in the middle of Comanche country."

"Yes and no. The Comanches have been pretty much cleared out by the buffalo soldiers and our Rangers, but San Bernardo has never had much trouble with anybody. It's like a little island in the middle of a tropical sea."

"Sounds mighty purty," I said, waiting him out.

"Don't be so skeptical, Sam." He chuckled. "The valley is mostly enclosed by mountains, so it's easy to defend. On top of that, a couple hundred years ago the original Spanish settlers made a peace with Comanches that both sides have honored for so long it's like a holy writ law now."

"So why do they need the Rangers?"

"They probably don't, but with the Indians moving west, so are the whites."

"They mean to build a fort there?"

"Maybe. Right now it's just a base camp where the Volunteers keep the pressure on the Comanches and protect the new settlers."

"Then why do they need a brand inspector?" I muttered, shaking my head.

"They don't. That's why it'll be just like a vacation." The commander beamed, his round face exuding equality, fraternity, and justice.

"I don't suppose you could just come out and say it plain as a wart on an old maid's nose what you're drivin' at."

He turned and rummaged through the pigeonholes of his desk until he found the letter where he knew it was all along.

The paper, smudged from handling, showed a kind of gothic, sharp-pointed handwriting that looked like it had been written fast and angrily:

Frederick Bell
Texas State Attorney General
Austin, Texas

Sir: As a Citizen of Texas and an officer of its courts, I demand that you remove the hostile, arrogant, iron-fisted overlords who pass as Texas Rangers from

30

the village of San Bernardo and the immediate area. A man has been murdered, and there will be more unless Captain Zanger is arrested, tried in a court of law, and hung for homicide in the first degree.

VINCIT OMNIA VERITAS!

Marcus Webb

I looked up at the commander, the question on my face.

"It was passed down to me from Fred Bell's office. Ogden Zanger is a very reputable officer, a hero of Chickamauga, a family man. He raised the battalion of Rangers Reserves. Bell doesn't know what to make of this crackpot Marcus Webb, so he asked for help."

"Why you?"

"Because we're outsiders and quasi-official. We can give an unbiased independent report."

"So you want me to ride out there to San Bernardo and just look over the Reserves and make a report. No arrests. No gunplay. Nothing."

"That's it in a nutshell." The commander nodded. "Call it a vacation with pay — and, I might add, the attorney general will pay a handsome bonus as well."

"What do you know about a murder out there?" I asked suspiciously.

"A man died in a rockslide. That's all there is to it." The commander smiled. "It happens all the time."

"Suppose my report confirms this jasper's letter?"

"You worry too much, Sam," the commander said. "It can't. You know the Rangers' reputation. It's impossible. Give yourself a chance to enjoy life for a change."

"I'd like that."

"Pick up your expense money, take Skofer along."

"Thanks."

Downstairs I stopped on the boardwalk to think about the assignment. I could still back out, but I had to think of Skofe and the practical matter of how to get from east Texas to central California.

San Bernardo was about three hundred miles west. Maybe we could just keep on going. Once I'd talked to Marcus Webb and Captain Ogden Zanger I could send in the report, and the commander could send my wages and bonus.

It was a dream. The commander was too smart to let me off that easy. He didn't just want his pound of flesh, he wanted a quart of blood, your horse, six-gun, sweetie, and a mortgage on your soul, too. He'd given me just enough money to cover our expenses going out and coming back.

Maybe in the weeks' ride to San Bernardo I'd come to terms with killing boys the way lawmen do.

The first killing, you got to go throw up, but after that it's easier and easier to justify the next ones, until you start walking straighter, blanking out your eyes, and sticking out your jaw, looking not for respect so much as admiration. "Look what a hard job I'm doin' every day riskin' my life killin' you folks for your own good. Ain't I the purple gingham flower of the prairie?"

It didn't work for me. Somehow I'd grown sicker and sicker with the killin', so I'd rather run than fight.

By the time I entered the Brindle Bull the sun had set, and darkness slowly followed along. Leap Malone, not famous for wasting either coal oil or whiskey, hadn't gotten around to lighting the lamps yet, which made the Brindle Bull about as cheery as a canvas outhouse in a blue norther.

Perhaps to cover their fear of darkness, men spoke in voices that were whispers, quiet as tombstones. I found the bar and made out the silhouette of Leap Malone.

33

"What'll you have, Sam?"

"I want some light first," I growled. "I don't drink anything I can't see."

"Sure thing, Sam." He hastily scratched a phosphor and touched it to a lamp wick. "You're sure touchy lately."

"I'm fixin' to take a vacation. Goin' to settle my nerves."

He poured me a glass of the Tennessee bourbon that you could take time to taste and not need to chase with horse liniment to keep from dissolving your vocal cords.

Malone went off to light the other three lamps in the place. On either side of me, scattered along the bar, I could now see the rest of the customers.

Most of them were working cowhands; the rest were dressed like politicians. At the front table I recognized a couple sporters in ribbons and bows, feathers and furbelows, velvet and satin, and several acres of powdered brisket.

One was new. She had her hair combed down over her forehead in ringlets, trying to hide the squint eye. She drank from her glass with her little finger stuck out like a gooseneck spur shank, and her bulging breastworks were modestly covered by a scarf tied in a bow. One tug and the gates to heaven would fall away.

34

The rannie next to me stared at that bow, licked his lips, then counted his change on the bar and shook his head despondently.

"Why the hell ain't there never enough money?" he grumbled.

The one on my right, a burly, stubble-faced stranger, looked me up and down and studied my face a second, then looked away.

The bottle in front of him was nearly empty, and the whiskey that had been in it was now weighing down the stranger's head.

"You're that damn stock detective," he mumbled.

"Steady on there, friend," I said quietly.

He frowned, trying to get his thoughts in line and moving.

"Bushwhacked all them kids . . ." he muttered.

"Wasn't that way," I said. "Best sleep on it, and we can talk tomorrow."

"Yellow. Scared to face a man face to face." He backed off a step. "Gutless, kid killer —"

The room became very quiet.

The burly stranger brought his right hand back to poise over his six-gun.

"You ready to face a growed-up man?" he asked loudly.

I raised my right hand with the glass high so his eyes followed it on up, and before he could make his draw I had the bottle in my left hand and swung it down on his wrist.

I heard a bone crack.

He stared at me with his hairy mouth open.

I grabbed him by the left shoulder and his belt buckle and in quick, fiery anger lifted and threw him out the batwing doors. He hit the slatted doors a little high and broke both of them off their hinges as he sailed out into the street.

It all happened so fast the sporters hadn't had time to duck, and Malone hadn't spilled a drop of the drink he was pouring.

"Damn it," I said, cooling off, "I didn't want to do that."

"Be glad you could," Malone said as the room settled down. "He didn't leave you much choice."

"I never bushwhacked anybody in my life," I said defensively.

"You goin' to worry about what every drunk says, you're goin' to age young," Malone said, and he went on down the bar.

I tasted the Tennessee again and felt better. Tomorrow I'd be out of it. Maybe I could get clean just ridin' open land talkin' to Skofe and my horse. Better I went alone. My horse made more sense than Skofer.

But he had a way of falling by the wayside

when I wasn't around, and if I left him in Austin he'd be swampin' out the Brindle Bull, sneakin' drinks and layin' in a corner like a damn old rat terrier with a tapeworm.

Where was he?

Likely passed out in the alley, I thought.

Off in the dark corner under the battered head of the brindle bull I made out a slumped form, but from what I could see, it didn't look like a man.

Over the raucous laughter of a group of satisfied politicians counting up their dirty business deals I heard a strange, discordant noise that sounded like a young rooster makin' his first crow, or an old lady gargling salt water.

"Seen Skofe?" I asked Malone as he mopped his way on by.

"In the corner." He nodded with his flushed bald head.

"Snoring?"

"I hate to say it, but he's playin' with himself," Malone said grimly, and he worked the gray rag on by. "If he wasn't your sidekick . . ."

I blushed. This was a side of Skofe new to me. We'd jumped some creeks together in the war and charged up some damn fool hills, too. We'd taken off our underwear and picked off the gray backs, and we'd howled around the cathouses a few times, but never anything like this.

I finished my drink and moved over to the corner, expecting the worst. Old Skofe sat on a chair facing the bull's head. He had the long curved ear trumpet poked in his left ear and the toy bugle in his right hand aimed right into it. His eyes were shut as he tried to blow a tune that sounded like a coyote with the croup.

"What you playin'?" I asked.

" 'Hell in Texas,' " he mumbled, not opening his eyes.

"I just doubt if there is such a song."

"Now that is the bale of straw that broke the pachyderm's vertebra." He nodded blearily to himself, his voice on the rise. "You asked for it, now you're goin' to get it the hard way!"

"Quiet down, Skofe. Malone's a little touchy tonight."

On wobbly legs he stood and looked at the bull, extended his arms eloquently to the battered and decorated head, and commenced singing in an earpiercing cracked tenor:

"O give me a bucket of bull blood,
Give me the prairie grass!
   You can take your oceans

38

And seafarin' notions
And stick 'em up your —"


"All right, you troublemakers!" Malone yelled from the bar. "Hit the trail! I run a decent establishment! Out!"

"Time to go," I said to Skofe.

"Who's that skunk breakin' wind like a fat bull goin' uphill?" he demanded.

"Out!"

"We're leavin'," I said mildly, taking Skofe by the collar.

"Bellerin' like a goddamned gut-gored buffalo —" Skofe screeched as I helped him toward the door.

"Out!"

"I'll sizzle his bacon!" Skofe snorted, trying to get a look at Malone.

"Out!"

"I'm the leapin' trout of the high waters, and I can whip any man in Texas!" Skofe yelled as we made it safely out through the broken doors.

"You shoulda let me teach 'em their manners," Skofe grumbled as we veered down the street toward the rooming house. "I'd have 'em whistlin' 'Sweet Adeline' over my backside in one easy lesson. . . ."

# 2

On the fifth morning out from Austin, feeling fine from being free of law and order according to somebody else, I put a pot of water on to boil and, looking through my saddlebag for the last heel of bacon, found Marcus Webb's letter.

"Take a look." I handed the letter over to Skofe and then commenced stringing slices of bacon on green willow switches to roast over the little fire.

"Sounds like he's short a few pieces of furniture in the upstairs parlor," Skofe said, studying the letter. "The Rangers are hard men, but I doubt you'd call 'em 'hostile, arrogant, iron-fisted overlords.' "

"What's that mean down at the end?" I asked, dumping a handful of ground Arbuckle's into the pot.

"*Vincit omnia veritas?* That just means 'Truth conquers all things.' "

"You reckon Comanches feel that way?"

"That's the way with old sayings. There's always one that'll make your case." Skofe smiled for the first time that morning.

"Like 'Boys will be boys'," I said softly, taking the letter and dropping it into the fire.

"You can't help it, Sam, if youngsters get guns and come up against you!" Skofer snapped. "Now get your head out of that gloomy cave and act like you're on vacation!"

We finished the bacon and coffee. I washed my hands again and mounted up.

It was the fresh kind of a morning, when you take a deep breath of the sweet-smelling air and you thank Providence you're alive. Thinking along those lines, I found my mood improved some.

Larks flashed from their nests in the grama grass like windblown golden leaves, red-winged blackbirds called out their business of the day from the wet sloughs, and an occasional flock of crows lumbered overhead, croaking, "Go back, go back!"

I decided the hell with it. I didn't want to be a sad old crow. I'd rather be a lark singing out the wonder of being alive in the world.

The past was past. Ahead were the hot-blooded señoritas, the calm, regular rhythm

41

of an ancient village by a river with all its problems worked out long ago. Ahead was some lazy fishing and hammock time under a shady tree.

You ride along after five, six days with nothing going on except the movement of your horse's shoulders under your hand, you have time enough to think about everything twice.

Why couldn't I just settle down to working full-time for the Stockmen's Association? Most of it could be just shuffling paper back and forth if I wanted it that way. I could have hired a man to go out and check that Lazy L brand that was being turned into a Hat. The commander would be retiring soon, and I'd move on up automatically. Then I'd retire, and the wheel would turn another time.

The fact was, I felt my work, in spite of the violence and blood, was better suited to me than farming or sailoring or chopping down somebody else's trees, which was like sayin' I wasn't different than anyone else.

The only difference, maybe, was that I meant to get back to California and raise cows.

"What are we goin' to do if we ever make it back to San Juan Bautista?" Skofe asked, reading my mind again.

42

"I reckon we'll just call on the widow Doña Encarnación at her rancho." I grinned.

"She might be married again," he said, chuckling.

"And widowed again" — I nodded — "and that would make it number four or five."

"Five," he said, "and that ought to tell you something."

The trail became more of an occasional wagon trace through the grass, and the country ahead looked to be more rolling and hilly.

"Reckon we're goin' to run into a war between the Texas Rangers and the San Bernardo folks?" I asked idly.

"Rangers are after hostiles and outlaws." Skofe shook his head. "Likely whatever bee was in Webb's head when he wrote that letter is gone and buzzed away by now."

The wagon trail worked around to the south and came up close to the San Bernardo River, which didn't amount to much this time of the year, and followed along beside it toward a sharp cut in a rocky hill to the west that looked to be steeper the closer we came.

Behind that hill rose a high red rimrock that would have stopped any wagon and most riders.

The wagon road turned as it met the deep, nearly dry streambed and followed its curve into the red sandstone cliffs rising gently, narrowing as the rock became more durable. I wondered if its builders had pinched it in because it would make the pass easier to defend or whether the rock was just too hard to move. Probably a little of both.

At the top of the rise the cliff opened up to give us a view of the green San Bernardo Valley.

I pulled up the steel dust and shook my head in wonder. After the rocky, parched trail we'd been inching along for five days the valley looked like a green paradise, an oasis nearly flat and nearly surrounded by red rock scarps like protective embattlements.

Just ahead of us was a dam that also served as a bridge.

Off to the right I could see the dammed upriver weaving off to the north, and at various points along the way irrigation ditches connected into the river and fed a patchwork of green fields and orchards and vineyards.

"Hard to believe there'd be a murder in a place that looks like heaven," Skofer said.

Ahead of us, across the bridge, I noticed a

44

neat arrangement of tents in a dried-out cornfield, and just beyond that was a very old village with narrow streets and adobe houses. On the left, but built close to the old buildings, stood a few new structures painted mostly white.

"The new and the old," I murmured, wondering how it had happened. It looked like the old had been slowly growing for a couple hundred years and the new had been set down overnight.

Old laurel trees shaded the central part of the old town, and at the far edge rose a hill that was dotted with small crypts and crosses painted a variety of bright colors.

Beyond the graveyard was a grassy open field where milk cows grazed, and on beyond vaulted the rosy red cliffs, topped by eroded pinnacles like castle turrets.

"I'm never goin' back to Austin," I said.

"Look before you leap from the fryin' pan into the stew pot. . . ." Skofer shook his head.

"Suppose we can just camp out under one of them big pecan trees by the river and fish and listen to the señoritas sing?" I asked, knowing that such a dream had never come true for me yet and likely never would.

"They've got grapes," Skofer murmured, licking his cracked lips. "That means they make refreshing spirits."

"Why don't you ever think of the finer things in life?" I muttered, and I nudged the steel dust into a slow trot on down the road.

A Lone Star flag drooped from a twisted mesquite pole in front of the tent encampment, and as long as we were supposed to be just strangers on the way west, I figured to play the part all the way.

"Maybe we better stop," Skofe murmured when he saw the sentries.

"I'm on vacation," I said, wishing it were true.

"Hold it up there, strangers!" the small sentry yelled, stepping out into the middle of the road, bold as brass.

I kept my knees tight on the steel dust just in case he had ideas of being shy, and at the last second the pint-sized banty rooster jumped aside. I was looking straight ahead, but I heard a new cartridge being levered into the chamber of the Winchester repeater.

I sat back, and the steel dust stopped.

"That's some more like what I want," the feisty little rifleman snapped out.

I looked down at him and wondered if I was going to have to kill him sooner, or later. I hoped never, for I was burned out playin' the Grim Reaper.

He wore a big brown hat, a cowhide vest with a new badge on it, and ordinary jeans. He had one of those faces some small men have who think they need to fight bigger men to prove something. His eyebrows were puffed and scarred, his cheekbones were padded with scar tissue, his nose bent off at an angle and was dented. A couple of his front teeth were missing, and his right eye was discolored from a recent encounter with a fist.

He'd lost a lot of fights. Probably thought it was his cross to bear, like his mission in life was to show that he might lose all the battles for his manhood, but he'd always come back for more. If he hadn't been so quick with the carbine, I'd have considered him pathetic.

I glanced over at the other one, a man obviously smarter than the runt. His face was broad and flat, with a heavy brow like a helmet coming down over deep-set eyes, and he had a jaw like a billet of pig iron.

The way he wore his duds made me suspicious because everything was oversize. It was like he was trying to hide his bigness by wearing a loose shirt, a long-tailed neckerchief, a drooping vest, and full-cut pants. It looked like it'd take him all summer to draw his Colt. Got to watch that one. He's already way ahead of you.

"Light down slow and easy," the battered runt drawled nasally.

"Looks like we crossed into a new country," I said to Skofe, who was climbing down off his roan like he was anxious to please.

I took my time because I wasn't so anxious. I was just starting the job that was supposed to be a little ride through the country.

As soon as I'd dismounted the runt came up behind quick, jerked my Peacemaker loose, and tossed it to the big man. Half a second later he jammed the muzzle of the carbine into the back of my neck and tried to sound like a grizzly bear.

"You dumb, or you just tryin' me out?"

"I'm dumb," I said.

"Figures." He chuckled. "Who are you?"

"Just a couple poor souls movin' west," Skofer quavered.

"You shut up, old man," the runt said. "I'm talkin' to this dumb son of a bitch."

I had read him right the first time and decided to sit in the game.

"We're searchin' you and your packs." The runt jabbed the Winchester into my back.

"Lookin' for something special?" I asked.

"That's none of your goddamned business, mister." The runt whipped the rifle

48

barrel back and brought it down on my right shoulder.

My arm went numb, and I felt sick to my stomach. I sank down on my left knee, stared at the dirt, and swallowed the flowing saliva until the sickness passed.

"They've agreed to the search, sergeant," the runt said, trying to sound like some kind of official in the military.

"Well done, Sidney." The other man spoke for the first time. "Watch that big one. He's still bronco."

The sergeant loosened our saddlebags and dumped our traveling goods out into the dust of the road.

I swallowed some more.

"Nothin' there," the sergeant said, poking through my spare set of clothes with his boot toe. "What's your business here, big man?" His voice changed to a harsh demand.

"Name's Sam Benbow. I'm just a broke-down cowman lookin' for a home."

"You may look like a cowman," the sergeant growled, "but you smell like law."

I shook my head and said nothing.

The runt was still behind me, and I had no warning when he brought the carbine barrel down hard on my left shoulder.

"Answer up!" Sidney snarled.

49

"I thought you was the law," I said, flexing my right hand.

"You got that right, mister." Sidney prodded the back of my neck with the carbine again. "We're Texas Rangers."

"That's enough, Sidney," the sergeant said.

"I always have respected the Rangers," I said, "but this don't seem like the same animal."

"You sayin' I'm a liar?" Sidney piped, ready to fight.

"I'm sayin' I was born in Texas, and I fought a good many years with General Hood's Texas Brigade, and you keep pokin' at me, I'm goin' to have to poke back."

"I'd call that a threat, Sidney." The sergeant laughed. "Poke him again and see if he means it."

I didn't wait for the barrel to jab me in the neck again because I guessed it was coming. I abruptly shifted to my left so that when Sidney shoved the barrel forward it went on past my neck where I hoped it would come, and I was already grabbing it with my good right hand.

Of course, when I jerked on the barrel Sidney's trigger finger dragged, and the bullet went by the sergeant's head as he dived for the ground.

Sidney tried to hold onto the stock as hard as he could, but I was coming up to my feet and turning toward him so that it jerked loose and was mine to have and to hold.

I brought my knee up into his belly to get him clear, then hooked a looping left across his face, bending his nose the other way.

I turned just as Skofer yelled.

The sergeant had a choke hold around my neck so fast I couldn't get set. I tried to jab at him with the butt of the carbine, but he moved aside and tried to bulldog me down.

He was heavy and powerfully built, and as I bowed my neck against the pressure he cut off my air and lifted his knee into the small of my back, and I felt my backbones begin to crack.

You can choke down a bronc with a lasso easy enough, but if you overdo it by just a few seconds, you'll end up with a worthless, mindless animal.

I was thinking about that as the darkness started to spin through my head like layers of black silk.

I felt myself falling, and I heard Skofer screeching, but it seemed like a good time to drop away.

"I was just doin' my job, captain."

"Sergeant Krimpke, I admire your zeal,

but not excessive force."

"Beg pardon, sir, but he nearly tore Sidney's head off. I had to subdue him somehow."

"Who are they?"

"They didn't have papers. That's what made me suspicious."

I recognized the voice of the sergeant, but not that of the captain. I wished I could hear Skofer's voice mixed in there someplace.

"Nothing on them relative to our problem?"

"Like I said, sir, they had no papers at all. It don't sound square to me."

My hearing faded away and drowned as the darkness flooded over again.

Next time, though, I heard Skofer's rasping, high-pitched voice rising and falling.

"My name is Skofer Haavik. I was born and raised in Charlottesville, Virginia, where I was professor of theology when the war started. I joined up under Jeb Stuart and after the war came to San Antonio, Texas, to make a new start."

"A new start is an old story for us," the captain said. "Why have you no proof of identity?"

"I'm who I am," Skofer answered. "I didn't know I needed papers."

"Your friend has no papers either. We

think that's strange. How do you make a living?"

"Cows." Skofer's voice faded in again. "But now we're travelin' west to greener pastures."

"You're well mounted, well dressed, well armed. You're not drifters nor poor, starved-out ranchers."

I flexed my hands and shifted my wrists slightly to make sure I wasn't tied up, then I opened my eyes.

"We quit before we starved out," Skofer was saying. "We've even got a little stake back in the bank to get us started when we find the right spot."

"What do you think, Sergeant Krimpke?" the captain asked.

"They're spies." The sergeant came right back. "Nobody uses this route to California."

Spies? What the hell was going on, I wondered. Why the search? Why the need for a proven identity? Why were the Texas Rangers worried about spies?

Because they weren't Rangers. They were an auxiliary bunch who'd never served as regulars. They were supposed to be volunteers fighting marauding Indians. Instead they had settled into this valley and, according to Marcus Webb, had committed murder.

Who? Why?

I was lying propped up on a cot inside a large tent. I could see Skofer and the sergeant off to my left, standing. In front of me, sitting at a desk, was a tall, big-boned man, maybe a little older than me. The tightness around his wide-spaced eyes reminded me of most of the survivors of the war, and judging by his stiff bearing, he'd served as an officer in battle.

"How do you feel, Mr. Benbow?" he asked me directly, catching me by surprise.

"I been worse."

"The sergeant was forced to use severe measures when you started swinging that carbine around," the captain said. "I'm Captain Zanger, chief of the Auxiliary Reserve Battalion of the Texas Rangers. Actually, the battalion is divided — half of it is in the north clearing out hostiles."

"We under arrest?" I asked, getting slowly to my feet.

"Technically no, but you are under our control according to the emergency powers act."

I'd never heard of such a statute, but I supposed the politicians had kept it stashed away for such time as they couldn't act legally.

"Sort of like you've declared your own

54

martial law in the San Bernardo Valley."

"The people of this valley are citizens of the U.S.A.," Zanger said. "But they choose to follow their own laws. I don't want you mixing with them."

"I think we'll just keep on ridin' west," I said, turning toward the open flap of the tent.

"I think you'd best stop at the Windsor House for a few days," Captain Zanger said smoothly. "I'd like some confirmation as to your business and identities before you leave."

"Afraid we're outlaws with bounties on our heads?" I looked back at Zanger. His expression was still as unchanging as a granite statue.

"I've no idea just now, but I agree with the sergeant that a traveler without papers is dangerous."

"Next thing you know the government will be brandin' babies' butts with big stars and stripes," I said to Skofer, and we went on outside.

The horses were at the hitch rail and the saddlebags replaced. I found my loaded six-gun in its belt hanging from the saddle horn and wondered why they were so all-fired salty one minute and sweet as honey the next.

As I mounted up Krimpke came out and said, "Windsor House is straight up the road. After you get through the old town you'll see it on the left."

In the short space between the encampment and the valley I saw that close to the ridge were vineyards, then an olive grove and orchards with a variety of fruit trees, from oranges and lemons to plums and peaches. Toward the center of the valley, on richer ground, were fields of corn and beans, squash, melons, and root crops. Where the most fertile soil was, tomatoes and cabbages, greens, cucumbers, onions, garlic, tomatillos, and chili peppers of several kinds were growing.

The people working in these fields with hoes, machetes, and pushcarts were small of stature and brown of skin, and they did not look at us directly as we passed by.

"Looks like they use every inch of ground they've got," Skofe observed.

"Where's their houses?" I asked, still grumpy.

"They probably live in town and push their carts out to their fields every morning," Skofe said.

The trail curved, and we saw the adobe houses gathered irregularly around the shaded central square. On down a ways clustered the few new buildings, bigger and taller, with more windows.

Very few people moved on the street, and no hot-blooded beauties moved anywhere. Little groups of children stared up at us with more hatred than fear as we rode by.

Along the way there was a cantina, a restaurant called Café Lupe, a general store, and little hole-in-the-wall *tiendas.* All quiet and peaceful.

*A man has been murdered and there will be more. . . .*

The plaza was big and green, with wooden benches and towering laurels and sycamores spaced around to give the whole park shade in summer. Across the way was a boxy little church with a simple cross on the roof. That was about it so far as old San Bernardo went, but on up a block were the newer, freshly painted buildings.

On the left was a two-story building with a sign that said First National Bank of Texas. Across the street was the Lone Star saloon. On the opposite corner stood a new mercantile where big-wheeled traders' wagons loaded and unloaded. Across the street was the New San Bernardo Café, and next to that a new building with a sign, WINDSOR HOUSE, ROOMS — BATHS. At the next corner a barnlike structure proclaimed itself as the H. Stegner Livery Stable.

"That's for me," I said, reining the steel dust over toward the livery.

We dismounted and, after stripping off our saddlebags, gave the reins to a lopsided old man with a stiff knee.

"You Stegner?" I asked.

"I am."

"How much to grain 'em and rub 'em down a couple days?"

"Fifty cents apiece."

I put a cartwheel in his hand and aimed for the Windsor House.

A heavyset lady with dark hair and a pug nose met us at the door. In spite of the summer heat she wore a full-length black dress of heavy bombazine.

Eyeing us sharply, she asked, "Rangers?"

"No'm," I said. "Pilgrims."

"Come in. I'm Mrs. Ada Kapp," she murmured, looking on past me at something in the street.

"A room and two beds, please, Mrs. Kapp," Skofer said politely.

"On the ground floor," she nodded, her attention still focused on the street. "Down the hall."

I eased my saddlebags to the floor and turned to see what was so interesting.

Two white men were coming our way

from the old part of town, and what was interesting were the armlocks they had on a pair of short Mexicans wearing white cotton pants and blouses.

The Mexicans were protesting in Spanish. The Rangers were responding in English, and they were all aiming for a blocky building with bars on the windows.

I stepped out on the boardwalk to get a better look.

The two Mexicans were trying to get their feet planted, but every time there was resistance the Rangers applied more pressure to the armlock, and off they went in a lunge that released the pressure until the Mexicans could get their feet set again.

I recognized Krimpke with another big Ranger slouching by the jail's front door, making jokes, laughing at the lunge-and-stop ambulation of the four men.

A few feet from the jail a small, skinny, sunburned man wearing a white blouse and pants, the same as the Mexicans, charged out of an alleyway and yelled, "Stop right there!"

He was bareheaded. His sandy hair fell to his shoulders. His teeth protruded at an odd angle.

I moved a little closer so I could hear better.

"Get out of the way, Marcus!" one of the Rangers yelled.

"Not until I know what this is all about!" the skinny young man demanded. "What's the charge?"

"These two is charged with loiterin' and agitatin'," the Ranger growled back, and he tightened up his armlock.

"You can't do this! You don't have any authority to lock people up!"

"We're just followin' orders," the Ranger replied. "Get out of the way."

"No, sir! Not so long as this is the United States of America!" Marcus Webb came back at him. "You've got to show me a valid warrant and legal authority before you can lock up any more of these people."

Krimpke lumbered over to Marcus and growled disgustedly, "Move out and shut up."

"Sergeant Krimpke, we've been over this time and again," young Marcus said, his voice coming down to a tone of reasoning. "You're a public servant. You simply cannot go around arresting people without proper authority and evidence of wrongdoing."

"I'm sure gettin' an earache from listenin' to your applesauce," Sergeant Krimpke muttered. "Now why don't you just be practical and save yourself a broke-up mouth?"

"I'm an officer of the court. You can't threaten me!" Marcus squeaked like he was astonished anybody'd talk straight to him.

"There ain't no court. Maybe we better lock you up for bein' crazy."

"These people have had their court and laws long before you were even thought of," Marcus squawked. "You're the ones ought to be arrested, you and every other Texas Ranger moving against this valley!"

"See! I knowed you was a loony. These people never heard of law'n order till we got here and showed 'em." Krimpke grinned and turned to the two Rangers. "Take him in for his own safety."

"No!" Marcus howled, and he pushed against Krimpke's broad chest to get away. "You can't do this!"

Krimpke let loose a looping right hand that smacked the lawyer in the mouth and dropped him like a swatted fly.

"Mister, you're a menace to yourself!" Krimpke smiled.

# 3

"Need any help, Sergeant?" I asked, stepping forward.

"Does it look like it?" Krimpke sneered,
rubbing his knuckles.

"Looks like a bad 'un," I said, trying to
divert the big man's intention of commit-
ting more mayhem, like delivering a kick to
the head.

"All mouth," Krimpke said. "One of them
legal eagles always stirrin' up things."

Krimpke was cooling off as Marcus pain-
fully got to his knees and looked at me, a
gleam of hope in his eyes.

"You from the governor?" he asked hus-
kily.

Krimpke's face froze. Suddenly he came
alert and turned to face me.

"What do you say?" he demanded.

"I say lock the dude up till he learns some
manners." I shrugged.

"Knew a feller back in Virginia" — Skofer

cackled — "and he was a talker! Famous for bein' a flannel-mouth jackleg lawyer. Name of Vincent Omar Veritas . . . that stump-sucker could get a town so stirred up . . ."

Jesus, I thought, Skofe, you damn fool idjit, why do you do these things?

But to give Marcus Webb credit, he broke off his stare quick when he heard that shaded Latin phrase.

"Just tell me, sergeant," he muttered, "what are you going to do to Morales and Higuera?"

"I figure to have a little talk with 'em about some property we been lookin' for. You want to be in on it, fine with me."

Turning back to the two Rangers who shoved the Mexicans inside, Krimpke said, "Lock him up."

Marcus shot a glance at us, but he went willing enough, and Krimpke turned back to me.

"Now, then . . ." He put on a smile like a crocodile eyeing a puppy dog. "What's this about the governor? Just who the hell are you?"

"You know my name, Krimpke."

"Havoc by name but not by nature!" Skofer stepped forward, a crooked grin on his old pinched face.

"Marcus knows you." Krimpke warily kept his attention on me.

"I never saw him before."

"Mighty nice little valley you've got here, sergeant." Skofer kept up his chatter. "Looks to me like it'll grow anything."

"Stubborn," Krimpke muttered. "God-damned mule-headed half-breeds is what it grows."

"If they aren't too grateful for your defendin' 'em against the Comanches, why don't you just leave 'em be?" I asked.

He cocked a sly look at me. "They got somethin' worked out with the Comanches. They trade and breed together. For all anybody knows, they're all cousins."

"People like that make us look bad" — Skofer nodded — "even though we've always tried to be peaceable."

"Except for takin' their land," I said.

"You got it wrong, mister." Krimpke glared. "It's everybody's land."

"Where's the dancing girls? I didn't come all this way to argue about a bunch of red-skins," Skofer put in quickly.

"Stay away from them," Krimpke said grimly. "You fool with their women, you're liable to get a knife in your back. Uptown's our place."

The other big Ranger guffawed. He was

bigger than Krimpke, and he wore his clothes tight. His shirt sleeves were torn off at the shoulder, showing his muscles.

"What the hell would an old pissant like you do with a dancin' girl anyways?"

While he laughed at his own joke I said, "Come on, Skofe, we haven't even looked at the room yet."

"Mighty exciting town!" Skofer started his chattering act. "Knife in the back, murder, searchin' saddlebags, stealin' property, Comanches and all . . . say, that's somethin' to write home about. . . ."

Krimpke looked at him, shook his head disgustedly, and went into the jail while I gently pushed Skofe back to the Windsor House.

"Any time you find one of them dancin' girls, just send her over to Griff Bletcher," the bare-armed Ranger sneered. "I like to make the sons o' bitches moan."

The way Skofer had tipped the feisty lawyer who we were put the whole job in jeopardy. Now that the lawyer was in Krimpke's big nutcracker hands I had little confidence in Webb being able to keep quiet if Krimpke wanted him to talk.

Krimpke in his oversized clothes trying to look small just meant big trouble. He moved deceptively fast, and he knew the killer holds and how to snap a short right hand with that extra wrist pop at the end of it. He probably had the left hook to match. On top of that, his sidekick, Griff Bletcher, was a gorilla out of his cage.

Worse, to me, was having to side with Webb. I didn't like lawyers — any lawyers — in the first place. The lawyers I disliked most had protruding teeth and long hair and tried to look like natives, while at the same time arguing about fine points of English common law just to make trouble for everybody in general.

What would that kind of hombre do if three kids started shooting at him? Would he shoot back or throw away his gun or demand a jury trial?

"Get it out of your head, Sam."

Skofer broke into my thoughts as we entered the vestibule once again.

The landlady sat in her rocking chair, frowning at her crocheting or whatever was ragging her mind.

"Have you been here long, ma'am?" I asked, picking up my saddlebags.

"Just a few months," she said quietly.

"No offense, but why did you pick this place to put a hotel?"

"My late husband's uncle has some money. He feels that New Bernardo will be the next Chicago," she said, not looking up.

"Where would he get an idea like that?" I asked, surprised, thinking somebody had to be crazy or have some information no one else had to leapfrog way out to hell and gone.

"Mr. Kapp said I didn't need to know, it was men's business," she said grimly.

I had a vision of her husband, Mr. Kapp, sitting at the head of the table, elbows out, eating his dinner alone while she served him.

"Yes'm," I said, and I followed Skofe down the hall. There was no carpet runner covering the varnished pine floor, and something in the air reproved our walking on it.

"Tread lightly, Sam." Skofer grinned up at me. "And don't feel so bad about stomping on horse manure."

Inside the room two single cots, one on either wall, left an aisle between, and at the foot of the cots stood a pine chest of drawers with a white ironstone basin and pitcher of water sitting on a crocheted doily. There wasn't a speck of dust. Hanging on a nail were two flour-sack towels.

"What am I doin' here?" I grumbled.

"Looking for a murderer," Skofe said sternly.

"We don't even know who was murdered."

"You can be sure it wasn't a Ranger or a businessman, or we'd have heard about it."

"That means it was one of the Mexicans."

"We surely need to parley with them," Skofer said, nodding.

I looked out the window and saw the clustered adobe buildings of old town, and right next to us, it seemed, were the new jail, bank, and saloon.

"I wonder if there's fish in that river," I said, thinking I'd like to be sitting on the bank yonder under a big shade tree watching a bobber drifting along.

"Sam Benbow, hearken to the voice from the cellar. We got a job to do," Skofer said.

"Ever since I rode off to war I been doin' jobs that were none of my doin', killin' men I never even knew. Now I'd kind of like to start lookin' out for good old do-gooder Sam."

"Later. In heaven, Sam." Skofer grinned. "But not now. Now the commander said go sort this noisy lawyer out of the chaff and see what makes him tick."

"I'd still like to know why they searched us."

"Whatever it is they're lookin' for, it'll fit in a saddlebag."

"That narrows it down some, all right."

"I suppose in the course of our investigation we ought to investigate the saloon," Skofer said, licking his thin lips and pushing his hat back.

He was already going out the door before I even agreed.

The Lone Star Saloon's pine floor was yet to come. For now it was smooth hard-packed adobe mixed with bull's blood or burned lime to make it hard enough to hold up under the star-heeled boots of the customers. The walls were ripped cottonwood boards that would curl up like a scorpion's tail as soon as they dried out. The ceiling was the underside of the plank roof that was covered with the same sort of hardened adobe as the floor.

The windows were just openings in the walls with wooden shutters. The bar itself was similar to the roofing planks except the timbers were thicker and planed smooth.

Maybe because the floor soaked up liquids and never needed mopping, there was the smell of riverbank mud, dank and rotten, underneath the usual smoke and sour beer smells.

The customers looked to be Rangers at one end of the bar, teamsters more in the middle, and citified dudes on the other end. I moved so we could stand between the teamsters and the dudes, keeping away from the Rangers on the general principle that I was supposed to be enjoying my work.

"Two beers," I said to the hulking bartender, who had a grimy apron tied around his alderman paunch so he looked like he was six months pregnant. His face was red, and his cheeks and nose blended into purple. His freckled bald head glistened with sweat, and the thick hair on his wrists and the backs of his big hands was red. Another Irishman.

Is it an accident the Irish always turn up behind the bar? Or is it part of their heredity? Maybe they are bred to bartending the way a border collie is bred to herd sheep or a bird dog is bred to sniff out partridges. Someday, I thought, I ought to ask Skofe about that. He'd know.

Naturally the beer was local, and because there were no hops out this way the brewmaster had used some other kind of flavor.

"Creosote bush?" I asked Skofer.

"Maybe willow bark." Skofe smiled. "That way you cure the headache at the same time you're making it."

"It's better'n a prohibitionist for teaching moderation. I hope you take the lesson to heart."

"Don't worry about old Skofe," Skofer

said expansively after only a half a glass of the stuff. "I can handle myself against old John Barleycorn, never you fear, lad."

"Sure, Skofe," I said. "Just remember the law around here seems to be Sergeant Krimpke, the hair-trigger type."

"You gents lookin' for work?" the tall, hump-shouldered man next to me asked straight out. "My name's Tom Durham. Bar D brand."

His lean, lantern-jawed face was burned dark brown and showed the sharp lines of sun squint and raw wind. Dressed in plain jeans, a flannel shirt, and a cowhide vest, he had all the earmarks of a range-riding cattleman.

He looked to be the only one of that breed in the whole place.

"Sorry, we're on our way to California," I said, thinking he knew we weren't going to work for him to start with, but he was tired of talkin' to himself, or he didn't like the answers he was gettin' back.

"I've got a thousand head of longhorns outside the valley and only four hands for help," Durham said.

"Mexicans make good cowboys," I said.

"Not these here. They're so lazy, they'd drown in their own dust."

"Maybe they're afraid of the Comanches,"

71

Skofer suggested.

"No, they get along with the hostiles somehow. If I don't get some help, I'm goin' to lose the whole herd in the next big norther."

"You've come west a little soon," I said.

"I like to get first choice of the water and grazing," he said. "There'll be a whole batch of folks rampagin' around here in another couple years."

"Can you wait that long?"

"I doubt it. These Bernardeños have been rustling more and more, and I can't watch my cows day and night."

"They're supposed to be traders and farmers. Maybe you could trade beef for cabbages." Skofer grinned.

"It's a helluva note when idle men won't work," Durham said harshly, his eyes cold. "I won't be sorry to see these Mexes cleared out and decent people moved in."

"Think it'll come to that?" I asked, surprised.

"How else can it be in this country?" he drawled.

"I was just wonderin' how they could be persuaded to move," I said. "We can pretty much handle the hostiles, because they don't have any papers or deeds or mortgages, but the Mexes here, they probably go clear back to some old Spanish king writing a paper sayin' this valley is theirs."

"I get your meanin', mister," Durham growled. "Now just where do you stand? For or against?"

"We're goin' to California and rook some Mexican widder woman out of a ranch," Skofer said owlishly.

"Why go all the way to California?" Durham asked. "Join up with me, and the sky's the limit."

"That's for sure, boys," the frock-coated, pot-bellied gent next to the cattleman said. "There's a fortune to be made right here."

"This here's B. G. Sharp," Durham said, stepping back and making room. "He's the new banker."

"I saw your building." I nodded to him. "Maybe you could tell me how come there is an old and a new San Bernardo."

"Simple enough." B. G. Sharp smiled like a gila monster eyeing a June bug. "The natives here wouldn't sell. Then one of 'em had an accident, and there was his field lying vacant, and we set up our own town on it."

"I guess he couldn't argue about it." I smiled.

The banker wore his gray hair so close-cropped it made his face look all the more like a red fox's, with wide cheekbones, hollows underneath, the jaw thin and narrow. His teeth were worn down so that his thin lips puckered in like he was getting ready to spit all the time.

"We've taken out the necessary applications for the land, don't worry," B. G. Sharp rasped. "The town is surveyed, plotted, and ready to ride the tide."

"No offense, sir," I said, "but I never heard of the town until a couple days ago."

"You will. The hub of the southwest, that's what we'll be. We've got water and flat land, and we're close to the crossroads north and south, east and west — everything that's needed for a great metropolis."

"You better listen to him, mister," Durham said.

"I haven't talked to anybody" — I beckoned to the bartender for another beer — "but it seems like them natives might put up a fight."

"Hell, the Comanches are tougher," the banker said, "and they're mostly wiped out by now."

"What about that rabble-rouser in jail?"

"His days in this town are numbered," B. G. Sharp said, looking foxier than ever.

"Did this wonderful plan spring from your own fertile imagination, Mr. Sharp?" Skofe asked, admiration overflowing his raunchy old face.

"I can't take all the credit." Sharp sighed. "Mr. Slade here, Alfred Slade, has been a big help."

"Pleased to meet you," the short fat man next to the banker said. "Alfred Slade here."

"Sam Benbow and Skofer Haavik here," Skofe said.

"Any time you need any legal advice concerning local property just call on me," the fat man said.

He wasn't just fat, he was fat the way a bear is fat in the fall, so his skin is stretched tight holding it all together. His hooded eyelids were fat. His ears looked fat. The backs of his hands were larded up with thick pads so his stubby fingers looked like tits on a bag-heavy cow.

"Mr. Slade is chief counsel for the Pecos Pacific Railway system."

"Don't think I ever heard of it," I said.

"You will, Mr. Benbow. You will," Slade promised, tipping up a small glass of amber-colored brandy.

"I'm beginning to understand the enthusiasm you gentlemen have for this beauteous place." Skofer smiled broadly, showing his worn-down biters, a dangerous sign that he was getting ready to elocute for an hour or two straight. "Railroads are the iron bonds uniting our great nation . . . purveyors of golden opportunities, benevolent, patriotic, and ever-generous, they serve as a model for the golden age of industrial expansion. . . ."

The room started to quiet down as Skofer warmed up to his subject.

"Railroads lead the vanguard of the revolution in swift and comfortable transportation. They are a boon to the farmer and the cattleman, the manufacturers and the common man!"

"Shut your tater trap!" a teamster about as big as his wagon yelled. "The goddamned railroad's hoggin' down the whole shebang, and what about us?"

"That'll do it, Mr. Haavik," I said, tugging at the back of his vest. "We don't want a riot on our first day in town."

"Your day has come and gone, my friend! Progress has overwhelmed the oxen and the cart, the mules and the drays, the horse and the wagon. The sunset of new ideas has fallen like a purple curtain across the stage of the whip and the goad —"

"You little bastard!" An ox-sized teamster made a blind lunge for Skofe.

I tripped him and kicked his ankle before he could get up, slowing him down, and was

76

hoping we'd have enough time to duck out the side door.

"You may crush my body, but you cannot hide from the dawning of the watershed of knowledge!" Skofe lifted his forefinger defiantly high.

When four teamsters and two Rangers rushed him he dropped quickly out of harm's way while the crowd above bumped shoulders and butted heads, which led to a teamster lifting a Ranger like a sack of beans and throwing him at the other, more peaceable Rangers in the corner.

Moderation and good sense disappeared. Rangers leapt forward to be swallowed into the vortex of milling, hammering adversaries while Tom Durham, Banker Sharp, and Alfred Slade slipped out the side door.

I'd have been glad to follow, but Skofer was tangled up in boots and chair legs, and I couldn't pull him free.

A gent with a flat nose like a bulldog's banged the top of my head with both fists. I jabbed my fingers in his eyes and brought my knee up hard into his crotch, dropping him down to Skofer's level.

I took an elbow in the ribs and a fist to the back of the neck, but I couldn't see who was responsible in the close-packed melee. Deciding one was as good as another, I started my own fight with whoever happened to come in front of me.

I hooked low and hooked high; I crossed my right to the kidney. I put the elbows in the ribs and brought the overhand down on a bearded jaw that slipped away. The next one in front had already started his right and clipped my jaw, waking me up to the possibility that a man might get hurt in this exercise.

I was getting arm-weary, and I felt somebody bite my leg. I stomped down and saw a light-skinned hombre on his knees ready to take another bite, and I brought my boot up hard into his sharp face. Then came the paired blasts of a double-barreled shotgun going off, and everyone froze.

My notion was that it wasn't the shotgun, it was simple weariness that really stopped the ruckus. The shotgun only made a good excuse to quit and have another drink.

The men gradually separated back to their places, all eyes on the purple-faced bartender, who was feeding two more brass shells into the open tubes.

I got Skofer by the back of the vest and lifted him to his feet.

He pawed away blindly at an invisible enemy, and I dragged him out the side door. Somebody laughed, breaking the tension.

"You can open your eyes now," I said, dusting the sawdust out of his thin gray hair.

"They're unwilling to admit the simple truth," he said sternly, puffed up with victory.

"What would that be today?" I asked, guiding him back to the Windsor House.

"The obvious fact that when you see a train coming at you, you're supposed to get out of the way."

"That's sensible, Skofe. Now maybe a cup of coffee and a porterhouse steak will brighten up the rest of your day."

"Wrong." Skofer patted the side of his head gently, making sure it was still safely attached to his neck. "We have work to do. We shall dine with the natives."

"No steak and mashed potatoes?" I shook my head with disappointment.

"No, *menudo.* Tripe soup. It is the archenemy of alcohol-induced neuralgia as well as a massive source of instant nourishment," Skofer expounded.

"Why didn't you think of that before we started drinkin' that creosote beer?" I asked, resigned now to the idea that the commander had known all along it was a hard job, and that to figure out the problem we'd need to hear the Bernardeños' side of it.

We left New Town and went down the

79

narrow street where the houses were side by side with an occasional closed door or window cut in the bare walls.

There were no children playing in the streets, only an occasional burro-drawn cart carrying corn or chili peppers to someone's house.

I noticed faces peeping over the half walls on the roofs. I supposed on hot nights the families slept up there.

The children's eyes were round, their mothers' wide and worried, their fathers' slitted. There were no cheery smiles.

"I get the feelin' we're as welcome here as ants at a church picnic," I murmured.

"And why not?" Skofer returned sotto voce. "They're not stupid. They know the train's coming, they just don't want to get out of the way."

I wondered if he had any idea of what he was saying.

A weathered sign said CAFÉ LUPE, and I leaned over to pass into a shadowed room where colorful hand-woven serapes hung on the walls along with colored engravings of saints, strings of dried chilis, and garlic bulbs braided together for good luck.

There was room enough for three tables and six chairs.

A girl, maybe fourteen, slim, lithe, and

ready to outrun us, appeared in a back doorway and stared.

A voice behind her murmured, and she stepped forward to make room for an older black-haired lady whose tall, abundant form belied the idea that all Mexican women are short and fat. Her fine features in the shadows reminded me of an alert deer, wary, testing, suspicious.

Beside her stood a tall, bushy-haired man in a suit and necktie and gold-framed spectacles. His long face was split down the middle by a long arc of a nose, like the leading edge of a platter or Death's curved scythe. Without speaking he came forward, tilted his head back, looked down his raptorial beak at us, and said in perfectly good English, "The café is closed."

"Sorry," I said, starting to turn away. "The door was open."

"*Pico,*" the lady said quickly, "*no está tu negocio.*"

"*Claro.*" He smiled blandly and made a short bow to her and added in an ironic tone to us, "She says my business is up at the school talking to blockheads."

"*No le hace,*" she said, meaning "Quit worrying," and she dismissed him with a curt nod of her head.

"*A tus órdenes,*" he replied with a trace of

sarcasm, and he backed out the door.

In the empty silence that followed Skofer faced the pair, took off his hat, and swept the floor with it as he bowed low.

*"Buenos tardes, señora y señorita."*

They stared at him bug-eyed.

*"Buenos tardes, señor,"* the lady said grimly. *"¿Que quieres?"*

Keeping his eyes on the taller lady, Skofer smiled and asked softly, *"¿Se llama Lupe?"*

*"Sí."* She nodded.

*"Por favor, Lupe, deseamos menudo."*

"Rangers?"

"No," I said.

Quietly and carefully she studied our faces. She stood like a hawk-faced judge weighing past experience against what she saw before her eyes. After a long moment she relaxed and nodded.

*"Bienvenidos,"* she said. *"Sentarse, por favor."*

We took her word of welcome and sat down.

# 4

The *menudo,* a rich broth in which pallid chunks of tripe floated, was brought out in large bowls, steaming hot. Along with the soup Lupe sent a stack of hot corn tortillas wrapped in a cotton towel. The girl served us while Lupe worked in the smoky kitchen from where we could hear the slap-slap-slap as she patted out more tortillas.

The girl, Marta, brought smaller bowls of chopped onion, cilantro, dried goat cheese, chilies, black olives, and spinach to be added to the *menudo* so that it became a meal in itself.

Toward the end Lupe brought us saucers of smoky fried beans topped with grated goat cheese.

With the beans served she took a chair between us.

*"Que sabrosa! Muchas gracias, señora,"* Skofer said, his health restored.

*"Por nada,"* she murmured, then she spoke

83

rapidly in Spanish, as if she had something on her mind.

*"Momentito, por favor"* — I held up my hands — *"mas despacio. No puedo . . ."*

She stopped in midphrase, smiled, then said slowly, one word at a time, "I have much English."

"Do you have much husband, too, Lupe?" I returned the smile.

"He is dead," she said coldly. "Them kill. Take . . . our . . . *tierra . . .*"

"The land over yonder?" I nodded over toward New Town.

"Was our farm," she added, her great dark eyes smoldering. "Now no more."

*"Tia!"* Marta said sharply. *"Son gringos!"*

"Marta," I said, "there are different kinds of gringos. We're not all skunks."

The girl backed away, not believing me.

*"Los hombres son caballeros como Señor Webb,"* Lupe said to her niece.

*"Está en el carcel!"* Marta shrieked bitterly.

Yes, he's in jail, I thought, and I wondered if Marcus Webb's enthusiasm for the Bernardeños' cause came before or after he'd met little Marta.

She had plenty of vitality and beauty to impress a young, romantic idealist from the east, and for a moment I regretted my own extra years that took me out of the race.

Good old Uncle Sam. I winced, seeing myself as the cartoon character: plug hat, gray hair, sharp nose, and pointed beard. A bumpkin clown.

I decided I'd rather be Uncle Ben. Good, kind, and portly Uncle Ben, the old gringo, helping young ladies find husbands while sitting in a rocking chair, smoking a pipe, nodding, spit leaking from the corners of his mouth.

Where the word gringo came from is lost in the fog of past times, but one idea is that it comes from an ancient verb, *grigar,* which meant what *grito* means today — a yell, outcry, loud clamor — words that describe us as we are seen and heard. We are noisy and rough. They are mellow and restrained except in moments of high passion, when often there is senseless killing.

I like a little of both, and the sooner we blend them together the better.

Lupe spoke rapidly to her niece in their own shortcut phrases that would take a lifetime to learn, and the girl dutifully faded out through the back door, but with anger clouding her fine-grained features.

"*Ai ai* — the young . . ." Lupe shook her head. "They think everything is simple. Black or white. All right or all wrong."

"You are lucky to learn differently at such

an early age," I said.

She blushed and looked at me. "You have honey on your tongue," she murmured with a little smile. "Have you a wife?"

"My sweetheart couldn't wait for me to return from the war," I said neutrally.

"When that happens it is difficult to find the innocence again." She nodded sympathetically. "I had good luck. Alfonso and I were very young when we fell in love. He was sixteen and I was fifteen when we asked permission to marry. Oh, the old ones were speechless, but no one was ashamed or unhappy. They wished us well."

She shrugged and looked me in the eyes. "He was a good man, but when we are born we know we must die."

"Do you have a chief, a head man in San Bernardo?" Skofer asked, changing the subject.

"Not really. We've never needed an *alcalde* or *delegado,* except maybe old Tio Ignacio. Tiburcio Bernal, the man who was just here, he has been educated in the east, but he is just a schoolteacher. Then we have our elders, too."

"You called him Pico." I nodded.

"It is a nickname." She smiled. "It means a big beak. Everyone jokes about it."

"It's a beautiful valley," I said, changing

86

the subject. "How many families live here?"

"Close to fifty," she said, pleased to talk about her home. "Not long after Cortez conquered all Mexico some soldiers, a priest, and some *carreteros* came here to baptize the Indians. They brought their diseases with the cross, and when the Indians died the Spaniards became colonists. That is why we are here. King Carlos of Spain signed our land grant, and we never give that up to anybody — bandits, *caciques,* emperors, nobody — including your General Houston or your Texas Rangers."

"Yet you are no longer citizens of Mexico," I said. "The treaty of Guadalupe Hidalgo made you citizens of the United States."

"I don't know much about those things, but Tiburcio Bernal does," she said.

"Are women permitted to speak of these things?" Skofer asked.

"Certainly — if they want to. Some want to and some don't. Nobody has to unless it is a time of great danger. We are very tolerant of all people, everything." She smiled.

As she spoke two men came in through the back door, followed by Marta. They both wore the simple white cotton costume of the Bernardeños and carried machetes in leather scabbards.

Lupe introduced the older man as Santos. Taller than average, he was thin and muscular and reminded me of a dried-out saguaro. His thin, sharp face was lined and hollowed, and his straight black hair was touched with gray.

"Santos is my cousin," Lupe said. "He grows the best corn and squash in the valley."

The other she introduced as her cousin Enrique, called Kiko for short. He was short and roly-poly and wore a long, fierce mustache that at first looked comical on his punkin face, but there was a disturbing expression of suspicion or hatred lurking in his deep-set eyes.

Neither stepped forward to shake hands.

*"Con mucho gusto —"* I made the standard polite greeting, but they were in no mood for politeness.

"What do you want?" the older man, Santos, asked.

"We want to know what is the problem here," I replied.

"Only problem is gringos. We want you all out," Santos said.

"We're on our way to California," I lied.

"You and those others" — Enrique spoke up — "you want our land."

"Not us," Skofer said, shaking his head.

"You mean the banker."

"All of you! Alfonso trusted them, and he is found dead under a rock. Your doctor called it an accident. We don't never have accidents like that," Kiko said fiercely, getting hotter by the minute.

"Steady on," I said, lifting my hands palms outward, "who do you think rolled a rock on him?"

"We believe he was beaten by Rangers," Lupe said calmly. "Maybe harder than they meant to, but it don't make any difference. He died. They took him over by the cliff and rolled some rocks down on him to make it look like an accident. I put a little cross over there."

"All right," I said. "Say you're right. Can you tell me why?"

"Because they thought he had the box with our papers," Santos said. "But he didn't ever have them. He would never tell who keeps the archives. They were very foolish, but that don't help Alfonso now."

"Would the box of papers fit into a saddlebag?" I asked.

The question took him by surprise, and he stopped to think before speaking. "No one has even seen that box for years maybe, but I would say yes, it would fit in a large saddlebag."

"What is this about saddlebags?" Lupe demanded angrily.

"The Rangers are searching for something," I said. "Probably that box. Tell me what happened after Alfonso's death."

"This is what happened!" Santos interrupted. "They took his and Lupe's farmland. They just started to build on it, and when we said no, it is not correct, they said, 'Prove it is yours.'"

"Can you prove your ownership?" I asked Lupe.

"Yes, but if we bring out the papers, they will just steal them, and then we will have nothing." She shrugged hopelessly.

"So you let it go while the people try to find a solution."

"The boy Marcus says law will come soon. Law with justice for all." Lupe nodded.

"Was Marcus Webb here when they came, or did he arrive later?"

"He was here. Just learning the language and going around studying the old paintings on the rocks and digging up things. He has money from back east."

"He says he is looking for real life," Kiko said. "We don't know what that means, but he never hurts nobody."

"And he's trying to help," Santos added.

"Also, he and Marta have an understanding. They are happy," Lupe said, looking at the floor.

"He is my *novio.* I am his *novia,* but we cannot see the future until the gringos get out," Marta said in a small voice.

"Now he is locked up," Kiko said. "Also, they have Joaquin and Timoteo with him."

"Do they have the archives?" I asked.

"It is impossible! No, of course not." Lupe shook her head with exasperation.

"Joaquin cleans the water ditches and sees that everyone has a fair share of the water," Santos said. "Timoteo is the man who does business with the traders for us when he's not raising chili peppers."

"Why were they arrested, then?"

"Because they don't hide away," Lupe said fiercely. "Because they don't bow and scrape. Because they walk with their faces open and their heads up."

"They mean to take us a few at a time so we don't get all mad together," Santos said. "We know what they are doing, and how, but we don't know why. We are not like Comanches attacking their people."

"Why are we trusting those men?" Kiko demanded. "They are spies!"

"No, Kiko," Lupe said, "I don't believe it. These two are different."

She looked me in the eyes and asked, "Do

you want something here? Land? Water? Money? A girl to make a blue-eyed baby with? Tell me, and you can have it."

"No, Lupe," I answered, "we want nothing here except peace and quiet. When we leave we will take only memories, good or bad, with us."

She looked from Kiko to Santos to Marta and back at Santos. "What do you think?"

"You don't answer the question," Kiko came back angrily. "Are you on their side or on our side?"

"I guess that's the real question," I said. "Maybe you better say something, Skofe."

"Please listen." Skofer took a long, slow breath and said, "We didn't come here to take sides. We came here to try and uphold the law. We have only your word that Alfonso was murdered, that the land has been stolen, that someone wants to steal your documents."

"You don't believe us?" Lupe asked quietly.

"As a matter of fact, I do," Skofer said, "but we need more than that. We need real proof that can be shown to the proper authorities."

"But you are going on to California," Kiko sneered. "You have nothing precious here to save."

"I don't want to sound too simpleminded, but we both believe in justice," I said, afraid to admit to myself that it was a pretty simpleminded idea most of the time.

"Pico's nose!" Kiko jerked his machete halfway out. "We don't want nothing but to be left alone!"

"The world is changing," I said. "You folks'll have to adapt to it."

"You mean give away our homes to the gringos and work as servants?" Kiko asked, getting mad again.

"You keep putting words in my mouth, friend, and that's not going to solve your problem. Better if you use your brains for a change."

I was sick of being picked on and bothered by his jerking his machete every once in a while like he figured that cutting my head off might relieve the pressure in his ears.

My experience has been that more harm is done in the world by sheer stupidity than sheer malice, but sheer greed tops them all.

*"Pinche cabron!"* Kiko yelled, jerking the machete free from its scabbard and lunging forward before anyone knew he was on the edge of going berserk.

I sidestepped a second before the machete came down in an arc that was meant to split me from stem to aitch-bone.

Whirling, he came at me again, the blade flicking from side to side as he tried to slice me crosswise.

I backpedaled fast as the tip of the blade ticked my shirt buttons, then I found myself with my back against a wall.

Driving forward, with his muscular torso backing up the machete, Kiko tried to impale me against the wall. I spun aside and took a scrape along my left rib cage as the blade jammed into the adobe.

Before he could yank it free I hit him in the back of the head with my right forearm, which served to slow him down some, and a half second later I had my feet set and put the leverage behind the right hand that caught him in the side of his fat neck.

He coughed, hawked, grabbed his throat, and sank to his knees.

I tossed the machete aside, then whacked the little round man on the back with the flat of my hand, which served to clear his windpipe. He sucked in a deep breath, then fell on his side, huffing and puffing, all the fight gone out of him.

He was a firecracker with a short fuse. But once he popped he was done and ready for a normal life all over again.

I lifted him to his feet and dusted him off.

"Kiko, we're probably on the same side,

but I have a different way of doing things than you do."

"It's not important," he whispered, "just don't call me stupid so quick."

"You're not stupid, you're just not thinking along the lines that will do you some good."

Santos had him by the arm, saying, "Come on, Kiko, that hot head will get you killed one day."

"I can't help it," Kiko said, shrugging. "It is Kiko."

"You can change," I said.

"No. There is where you're wrong. Mexicans don't ever change."

"Thank you, Lupe, for a grand meal," Skofer said before tempers rose again. "And it has been a pleasure talking to you." He turned gallantly to Marta. "And you, *hija,* we will do what we can to release your *novio.*"

It took a while to disengage from their flowery farewells, but about five minutes later we made it into the street and turned back toward the rooming house.

The sun had set over the rigid western scarps, and twilight was yielding to darkness, but the town was small enough so that you could walk up the middle of the street and not bang into anything. At the end where New Town started both the saloon and the hotel across the way were lighted by coal-oil lamps.

"Drink?" Skofer asked as we trudged along, thinking our own dismal thoughts.

"Not me. I'm tired from playing mumblety-peg with Kiko," I said, not mentioning that my side felt like I'd ridden through a thorn patch.

"You handled that with perception," he said. "I was a bit worried you'd broken his larynx."

"If I'd hit him more to the front, it would have killed him. It's a fine point I generally try to avoid."

"The main thing is that he carries no grudge."

"If I thought he was that kind, I'd have shot him," I said. Then I saw the three boys with the running iron — saw the youngest on his back, the red bubble growing on his mouth like death's toadstool. . . . You old bastard . . . !

We entered the Windsor House and found Mrs. Kapp in her rocking chair, crocheting by the dim light of a lamp.

She glanced at us as we came in, but her fingers kept moving the crochet hook. "Have you had supper?" she asked.

"Yes'm," I said.

"I saved some fried liver."

"Sorry, ma'am, maybe you can grind it up tomorrow and make liver loaf."

"It's still hot," she persisted.

"I reckon we're full, ma'am." Skofer took over while I went down the hall.

"You might have let me know."

"We didn't figure you meant for us to eat here, dear lady. Please don't count on us for regular meals."

"Are you not regular men?"

"Yes and no, Mrs. Kapp." Skofer had decided to give her both barrels, and I tarried by the door to hear him carry on.

"You see, when I was a boy growing up on the Roanoke River my mother always told me never to eat any of the various creatures I often came across, such as bloodworms, tadpoles, frog eggs, and rock lice."

"You didn't eat any of that stuff, did you?"

"Not that day. I had to curry my pony and skim the cream and fill the woodbox, chores a small boy normally does. But the next day I was free for a few hours, and about noon I found a strange critter like a gooeyduck clam in the riverbank. Caught him so quick, he hardly had time to squirt me in the eye. There he was, a nice rasher of meat on one end, and then his big long neck hanging

97

down. . . ."

"Please, Mr. Haavik," the plump, dark-haired lady protested, no longer moving the crochet hook.

"I'll finish in just a second," he said hurriedly. "Well, I tried to tear him up into small pieces, but those gooeyducks, they're too tough to tear, so I thought I could just chew him to pieces before swallowing him down. That almost seemed to work as I chewed away on the bottom, meaty part of him. I chewed and chewed with the neck still hangin' down about to my belt buckle, and without thinking about it I swallowed most of it down, which still left about an inch of it poking out of my mouth.

"I chewed and chewed, but it's near impossible to chew through the neck of a raw gooeyduck, so I ran home, expecting my mother would have an easy solution.

"Somehow I managed to attract her attention and slobbered out, 'Mama, how do you eat one of these darned things?'

"Well, of course she saw the clam neck sticking out of my mouth like it was the hind end of a snake, and she fainted dead away."

Skofer nodded as if the story were finished, and Mrs. Kapp waited a moment before asking, "Well? Did you cough it up or swallow it down?"

"It just slid down by itself," Skofer said, nodding, "and as far as I know it's still down there somewhere. That's why I don't have an appetite like regular folks. I have to wait until that gooeyduck down there gives me a nip and tells me he's ready to eat my dinner."

Mrs. Kapp put her crocheting aside, still staring at Skofer, lifted the lamp, and said, "Good night, Mr. Haavik. You need not eat at my table."

As she marched up the stairs I went into the room, fumbled around, and got a phosphor going so I could find our lamp. I touched it to the wick, fitted the globe back into the prongs, and turned to meet Skofer coming in the door.

"How come you scarin' that poor woman half to death? She'll have nightmares all night long."

"She shouldn't have tried to nag," Skofe said without cracking a smile.

"You have no conscience," I said, taking off my shirt and washing the scrape on my side with a wet towel.

"Maybe not, but I'm the only one around keeping a real live gooeyduck clam for a pet!" Skofer crowed.

"Been a long day," I said tiredly, feeling

an unconquerable drowsiness coming over me.

"Pretty good for starters," Skofer said, prying his boots off, blowing out the lamp, and turning in.

I saw the dusty, beardless face, the splayed-out yellow hair, the bitter eyes, and heard him retch out *'You old bastard . . .'* but it was different because the guns were still going off. I couldn't fit them into the recurrent nightmare. There should be only his last rushing curse, yet there were yells, boots running on the boardwalk outside, and more gunfire. . . .

I moved the big cube of darkness that was weighing me down until I could see around it and said, "Wake up, Skofe."

I lighted the lamp and slipped on my boots. I'd gone to sleep so fast I was still dressed.

Skofer groaned, "Tell me —"

"Shooting over towards the jail. Sounds like a damn battle out there."

"The jail," he repeated, when we both heard a stumbling thudding in the hall and a little moan pulsing at regular intervals.

Skofer opened the door and I caught young Marcus Webb as he fell.

Bringing him on inside, I turned him over on his back. Blood was spreading out in a

100

pool from two bullet wounds. His face looked like he'd been staked out in a mule pen.

"*Vincit,*" he said, looking up at me, biting his swollen, smashed lip.

"*Omnia veritas,*" I finished for him.

"*El Punto,* remember!"

"*El Punto* what?" I leaned over and put my ear close to his lips.

"*Veritas . . .*" he whispered, and a shudder ran up his body from his toes to the top of his head. His head flopped sidewise, and I backed away.

"Backshot," Skofe said.

"Just a youngster," I said. "God damn it."

# 5

"Hold it right there!"

I turned to see Sergeant Krimpke, Griff Bletcher, and two more Rangers charging through the door, their six-guns at the ready. Krimpke's beefy face was flushed with blood lust, his eyes wild.

"Back up!" he yelled.

"Steady on, sergeant." I lifted my hands and backed away from the body. "He's dead."

Krimpke glared down at the lifeless form spread out on the varnished floorboards.

"What did he say?" he growled.

"He wanted to know why you shot him in the back."

"They busted out of jail. It was dark. And it looks like you helped break him out."

"We didn't even know him," Skofer said in a small voice.

"We're goin' over to the jail and get the straight of it," the sergeant growled.

"Mister, we're not goin' anywhere with you," I said firmly.

He raised the Colt .44 casually, and I heard a hammer cock behind me. My own six-gun and gun belt lay on the table, a lifetime away.

"You goin' one way or another," Krimpke said harshly.

"We can walk," Skofer said.

In the dim dawn we went out into the street where the early risers silently stared down the alley behind the jail.

"All three?" I asked, feeling sick.

"Somebody from the outside pulled the bars out of their window. I yelled at 'em to stop, but they thought they could outrun a bullet."

"Sounds like a turkey shoot," I said.

"I want answers," Krimpke said, herding us into the squat adobe building. "Maybe your partner can remember what he had for dinner yesterday."

So he knew we'd talked with Lupe, and maybe he knew Santos and Kiko had dropped in the back way.

Why were they keeping an eye on us?

Nervous.

"Griff, take the big jasper back and show him the busted window while I have a little talk with this old gent," Krimpke said to the

103

man behind me.

"Just a second," I protested until I felt the barrel grind into my back.

"I'll be okay, Sam," Skofer said in a small voice. "These boys mean well."

Skofer was shoved into a small room that served as an office, and I was pushed on down the hall to the back room that had been converted to a cell.

There were two bunks in it and not much else. The bars in the window had been pulled out by somebody on a horse with a rope.

You ride up close, pass your reata around the three bars, dally on the saddle horn, and knee your mount forward. The dry, brittle adobe has little strength in it. It is good to keep the heat, snakes, and bugs out, but to hold anything it needs reinforcement.

The hole was big enough for a man to wiggle through. I wondered if they'd known their liberator. I wondered if they'd considered that the whole thing was a trap made for their legal execution.

For sure the kid had been beaten so badly he'd be ready to grab any straw to get free.

Why would they mash him up so?

*El Punto?* Meaning the point, the crest, degree, period. Sometimes it means a hole in a sock or a net. *Punto* had so many shaded meanings you couldn't pin it down.

I went into the cell and crumbled a loose clod of adobe between my thumb and finger. Griff Bletcher lumbered back up the hall like a Kodiak bear.

A man could damn near claw his way through that wall if no one was watching. But of course it hadn't been built to be a jail; it was probably only meant to be Alfonso's storeroom until Krimpke had commandeered it.

I heard a curse and a small, tight shriek of pain from up the hall.

I turned quickly and saw two younger Rangers filling the door, their Colts leveled at my middle.

"Take it easy, big fella," one of them said. He had peach fuzz for a beard and big yellow buck teeth that looked like they'd better fit a mule.

"That's my partner!" I stepped forward.

"Likely he fell down." The other pimply-faced razorback kid grinned.

"Don't do nothin' crazy. Boss said he wanted you alive," Mule Teeth said. "Said if you got fractious, blow your hand off or mash up your knees."

"Don't you boys believe in a day of reckoning?"

"You mean when we go knockin' on St.

105

Peter's gate?" The razorback kid smiled.

I heard Skofer groan tightly, holding in the worst of it.

"No," I said, "when I come knockin' on your door."

"We don't have no door," Mule Teeth said. "We got nothin' but thirty a month. That ain't much to lose."

"I was thinkin' more about a hard dyin'. You can count on it if you let that crazy son of a bitch beat an old man."

"We better remember that, Rafe," Mule Teeth laughed, "when we're hangin' this jasper in the town square."

Suddenly the door to the office burst open, and Skofer came staggering out with Krimpke and Griff Bletcher right behind him. Blood leaked from Skofer's mouth, and one eye was half closed.

"Wash him up in the horse trough," Krimpke said, "and keep him close by."

With one big hand Bletcher half carried, half dragged Skofer out the front door as Krimpke turned toward us.

"Bring that big pine tree in, and let's see if I can bark him some," Krimpke said.

"Move," Mule Teeth snapped, stepping clear of the cell door.

"Make a wrong move, mister, I'm goin' to mash your knee first off," the razorback called Rafe said, reading my mind.

With hard-heeled boots knocking, Krimpke went in ahead of us and had his six-gun drawn and ready when I came in.

"Mad, ain't you? Want to fight, don't you? Well, so do I, but I got a job to do, and you're goin' to help me do it. Set there."

He pointed his gun at a chair with a cowhide seat while Mule Teeth and Rafe kept their positions on either side, waiting for me to lose my temper.

I sat.

"You're smarter'n you look," Krimpke grunted.

"You didn't need to bust up that old man," I said. "I won't forget it, either."

Krimpke poked his gun barrel against my jawbone. "Shut up!" He turned the barrel and pulled it down so the sight made a scratch across my jaw.

"The old man is goin' to get a lot worse if I don't get some right answers damn soon."

"You know everything we know already." I shrugged.

"I want to know what that flannel-mouthed lawyer was doin' in your room."

"He was dyin'," I said. "It took him a hard half a second."

"What did he say?"

"Sounded like he said he wanted a jury

trial, but it was probably somethin' else."

"Your partner said he never said anything," Krimpke snarled. "Goddamnit, save yourself a lot of pain and spit it out."

"Maybe it was 'Poor folks have poor ways,' or 'Lots of fleas on a lean hound.' I didn't catch it."

"Why was he there?"

"I didn't know him. Skofer neither." I shrugged.

"He had a reason. Maybe they got word to him that you'd been talkin' to the Mexes."

"We ate dinner in a café."

"You lyin' bastard. I know that greasy Santos and his buddy Enrique came in the back way. What did they say?"

"As near as I could understand, they said they hated noisy gringos," I replied quietly, my temper cooling off so that I could think clearer. "One of 'em tried to take his machete to me."

"That damn fool Webb said he sent for some special agents. He shouldn't have done that. The Rangers have everything under control. Are you workin' for the governor?"

"I figure governors are about as low as Rangers. I don't like him any more'n I like you."

Krimpke glared at me, his deep-set eyes boring in, upper lip twisted. "You're goin' to talk yourself to death just like the legal eagle." He holstered his six-gun and slipped a glove on his right hand. "When I hit you, your brain is goin' to bounce against your skull. I'm goin' to hit you until your brain is curdled up like pot cheese. Maybe by then you'll give me some simple answers to simple questions."

"I didn't know that kid. I don't know the governor. I just want to go to California. That's the truth," I said as he swung.

I tried to duck, and instead of taking the fist on the chin I took it just forward of my ear.

He was right. The brain bounces against the liquid padding and smacks against the headbone.

Takes something out of you.

I tried to rise up from the chair, and the young Rangers grabbed my arms. His next right hand landed where he wanted it.

"Anytime you want to talk, just sound off," he growled, already breathing heavily.

Next time his fist hit right square on the cheekbone. I tried to roll and dissipate the force of the blow, but he didn't like that and hit me again in the same place to make sure it was well covered.

My mind was going out and coming back, going out and coming back, like raising and lowering a burning lamp wick, and I finally got the notion that Krimpke wouldn't mind making mush out of my brains whether he got any answers or not.

"The way it was," I said, just to stop the next right cross that I figured would be my last, "the way it was, Skofer and me, we . . ."

I was trying to think of something that'd make him happy enough to grow careless, but my old onion wasn't working too well.

"It started when some kids tried rustling the Lazy L cows. We wasn't involved in anything until . . ."

"Until what?"

I figured if I couldn't find an answer right quick, I'd better change my ways.

"Until what?"

. . . How should I know? Until the cow jumped over the moon. Until hell freezes over . . . until death do us part . . .

Rafe and Mule Teeth were relaxing their holds as they waited for me to finish the until.

"Until . . ."

Nothing for it but to buck backward, jerk up both boots, and kick Krimpke in the belly, then grab Rafe and Mule Teeth by their necks as I came back forward, smack-

110

ing their heads together enough to slow them down some.

Leaping clear, I crossed my own right on Krimpke's jaw as he started to draw his six-gun, then whirled and kicked Rafe in the kneecap and felt it shift around a quarter turn. He screamed and fell.

Mule Teeth landed his overhand right on top of my head, but before his left came over I hit him in the face with Rafe's hat, then ducked down, grabbed his ankles, and heaved him over my shoulders so his head bounced off the back wall. Krimpke was coming back, and I crossed the same right again, splitting my knuckles this time, and I wished I'd had a glove on.

Rafe shifted as he tried to rise, and I pulled his six-gun free.

I was backing out the door when I felt the unmistakable iron bore of an army Colt in that little cleft above the bottom backbone.

"Drop it, Mr. Benbow," came the crisp voice of Captain Zanger.

"Why?" I asked, holding my own weapon steady. "So these polecats you call Rangers can butcher me slow?"

"They will not harm you in any way," he said coldly. Changing his voice to a harsh command, he barked, "Is that understood, sergeant?"

"Yes, sir," Krimpke replied sullenly.

"Say that again, sergeant!"

"Yes, *sir!*" the sergeant said quickly.

"I'll have you flogged with a bullwhip before the entire command if you ever disobey my orders again, understand?"

"Yes, *sir!*" The burly sergeant stood straight at attention, his eyes looking through the top of his head.

"I will want a full report of this disgraceful scene, sergeant. Now clear out of here."

"Yes, *sir!*" Krimpke snapped. He stepped by me and the captain and went out the door, followed by a wobbly Mule Teeth and a limping Rafe.

The gun barrel left my back, and I turned to look at the tall captain, whose eyes were like icicles at forty below.

"My partner?"

"I met him outside. He's at the hotel now. I've sent for the doctor. Please sit down."

I went back to the chair, and he sat behind the desk.

"I want to express my sincere apologies for this sad affair," he said slowly, studying the desktop, then looking up at me. "I hope you've not been seriously hurt."

"I'm glad you showed up."

"These men haven't the discipline of the regular army." He shook his head thoughtfully. "I suppose you served?"

"I had four years of it. That was enough."

"I was invalided home in the winter of sixty-three," he said. "Took a shell fragment — just a sliver, thankfully — through the lung."

"Not many survive those."

"It was a sucking wound that wouldn't heal for months." He nodded. "My dear family nursed me back from the brink of death."

He talked like he'd read the words in a book, all formal and polite, careful, planned.

"But let me not digress on my own personal affairs," he said abruptly. "I wish to explain to you my mission so that perhaps you can understand what's happening here."

"I've been wondering."

"Very well. My orders are to protect the San Bernardo Valley and all people in the vicinity from hostiles, principally Comanches."

"The Comanches are all but finished. They're reduced to boys with bows and arrows."

"There are still many settled more or less in the Nations. They may break loose whenever they feel like it."

I didn't agree, but there was no point in arguing. According to my information, the

Comanches had become starving beggars hanging around the Indian Agency slaughter pens.

"My secondary mission as outlined by my superiors is to make sure the immigrants who wish to settle here are given equal opportunities."

"That sounds like some of the legal eagle kid's speechifyin'." I smiled.

"Indeed. They make my orders so vague that no matter what I do, it can be interpreted as being good or evil. That is the civilian politician's means of self-preservation."

I nodded, letting him get on with it.

"Compounding the problem is the quality of my troops. They are little more than desperadoes. Undisciplined, ignorant renegades, most of them. If I had not sworn on my oath to do my duty, I would resign immediately and take my family back to South Carolina."

I was beginning to understand the dilemma of the ramrod-style officer. He was commanding rabble, deserters, bounty jumpers, bummers, pukes, and plain outlaws.

"Maybe you ought to let the governor know what's goin' on," I suggested.

"And admit that I'm not competent to

command these troops? No, sir, I will command them. It's going to take some time to whip them into shape, but I will!"

"That's the only idea I've got to offer," I said, starting to rise.

"Wait, please, Mr. Benbow. You've been a soldier. You understand the ways and means and wherewithal. Would you consider joining up with me and taking charge of companies D, E, and F?"

"I'm on my way to California, like I said." I shook my head. "We only stopped to rest the horses."

"I do not wish to impose on you, sir." He nodded. "I wish you a safe trip."

Frowning, he inspected his fingernails, ran a rag over his shiny boots, then looked up at me and added, "There's something else you might help me with if I'm not asking too much."

"Go ahead," I said neutrally.

"The young Yankee rabble-rouser I understand was killed while attempting to escape from jail. Can you tell me why he wanted to break out?"

"I believe he thought the man named Alfonso was beaten to death by your men," I said quietly.

"That is not possible!" Zanger exclaimed. "Alfonso Madrigal was a bit bruised, but no more than you are. I know he was alive and able to walk when he was released."

"I'd like to know why Marcus was arrested."

"Frankly, he'd been disrespectful to the Americans here, and he was inciting the natives against us with false accusations. The specific charge against him was interfering in the arrest of the two natives who are now also dead."

"What had they done illegal?"

"They were suspected of rustling cattle from a rancher named Tom Durham."

"Evidence?"

"A wet hide with the Bar D brand hanging in their outbuilding."

"Could have been a plant," I said, "but it's not my business."

"The young man had some special knowledge he was using against the whites. Could you tell me anything about it?"

"I didn't know him. Never met him until he died at my feet." I shook my head.

"That's it," he said tiredly. "I wonder if you'd do me the honor of having dinner with me and my family today. I'd like to show you that we're not all so disreputable."

"Depends on my partner's health."

"Very well. We dine at one. My family is temporarily housed in the town's meeting hall down the street, which we've converted to basic accommodations."

He stood and extended his hand and tried to make a smile. "Thank you for your patience, and please extend my apologies to your friend as well."

I shook his hand and, turning away, said, "I'm feelin' some better about the Rangers, thanks to you."

I hurried back over to the hotel and found Skofer in the room, lying on his cot with a fuzzy-sideburned medico seated alongside.

Skofe's right eye was almost swollen shut, and the side of his face had a couple lumps on it, and I began to get mad again.

"My — ain't you a sight!" Skofer beat me to it. "Your face looks like a bagful of river rocks."

"Just one side," I said. "Anything broke?"

"Hurt my pride more'n anything. I gave him a good punch to the jaw, but my fist just bounced off. He laughed like it was quite a joke." Skofer frowned. "Then he said, 'Let me show you how.' "

"If it'll make you feel any better, the captain promised him a flogging if there was any more of it."

"I'd rather the fact than the promise," Skofer said.

"That's enough," the doctor said in a

Germanic accent. "I am Doctor Heinrich Daud. This man is not so young anymore. He needs rest after such a beating."

Skofer closed his eyes. "I ain't that old."

"That'll be ten dollars," Daud said.

Skofer seemed to stiffen and rise off the bed horizontally. "Ten dollars! You ain't even been here five minutes! I can get ten horses shod for less'n that!"

"My dear sir," Dr. Daud said, "you must understand that I had to study several years to become a doctor. A blacksmith never has to sacrifice his youth for service to mankind the way doctors do."

"Ten dollars!" Skofer howled again.

"Sorry, Doc," I said, "I'll have to give you an IOU."

"No, sir, I cannot buy expensive drugs and instruments with IOUs." His face reddened, his voice losing the honey he'd wasted his youth learning.

"Maybe you can make it up from somebody else that's worse off than Skofe," I suggested.

"Suppose that you need a doctor again. Do you think I will leave my hot hassenpfeffer to save your life?" he grated coldly.

"I guess we'll have to chance it, Doc. Would a dollar help?"

"I could have you both arrested," he

blustered, his white sideburns flapping like moth wings and releasing a faint cloud of talcum powder.

"We've done tried that," Skofer said.

"I'm due for dinner at the captain's house," I said.

"Pay me the dollar," Daud said.

"Changed my mind," I said, "but if you get hurt, I'll leave my jackrabbit stew to come help you."

"That sounds square to me," Skofe said.

*"Mein Gott in Himmel!"* The dedicated Dr. Daud smacked the back of his hand against his forehead like he had the slobbers or the ziggers. "I am a practicing physician!"

"Afraid you're a gouger, too." I nodded. "Don't be downhearted, there's a plenty more just like you."

He grabbed his black cowhide bag and hustled out the door yelling, "You haven't heard the end of this, I promise you! I'll spread the word, and no doctor will ever touch you!"

"Suture self," Skofer said, not cracking a smile as the door slammed.

"I wish I'd said that." I laughed.

"You really goin' to visit the captain?" Skofer asked.

"Him and his family," I said. "Want to come along?"

"No. I've got a bellyache and a twisted knee. Maybe after a nap it'll turn out to be a bad dream after all."

"Afraid not. There's three dead men that aren't goin' to wake up, and all of 'em were shot in the back."

"The captain in on it?" Skofer asked, closing his eyes.

"Hard to say," I said softly. "He seemed mighty sorry about our troubles. Wanted me to be his adjutant and whip the troops into shape."

"Tell me, Sam." Skofer closed his eyes and sighed weakly. "Does a doctor doctor a doctor according to the doctored doctor's doctrine, or does the doctor doing the doctoring doctor the other doctor according to his own doctoring doctrine?"

# 6

The town hall of San Bernardo looked like an ancient pile of whitewashed adobe bricks with ragged bits of straw poking from the eroded mix.

The tall, narrow doors were made of oak planks, and the iron strap hinges had been forged by a long-dead blacksmith in a long-dead charcoal fire.

The knocker was an iron fist hung on a ring, and I rapped twice with it. I wondered if everyone in old San Bernardo heard that rapping and knew it meant I was to break bread with the invader.

The lady who opened the door was not tall, but she stood straight with her shoulders back like she'd been well drilled. I saw that her face, though once lean and handsome, had become tremulous and haggard.

"Mr. Benbow," she said, "I'm Rose Zanger. Please come in. We've been looking forward to your visit."

She spoke the polite words properly, but there was a weariness in her that blurred the edges of her speech.

The floor was worn terra-cotta tile, and the walls were plastered and whitewashed adobe. It was a large room, and the roof was supported by heavy logs. A long, hand-hewn and -planed oak table and a number of simple chairs with ladder backs and cowhide seats occupied the right side of the room, while the left side was more of a parlor, with imported vases and dried ferns, brass candlesticks on walnut tables, Venetian glass birds, and imitation marble nymphs and cupids.

Doors led off the main room to left and right, and to the rear was a special double door with small glass panes fitted into it.

"Please come out to the patio. Everyone is gathered there." I followed her through the paned door into a central open area with dirt paths running through a garden of roses and lilac bushes, and clumps of lilies that had already bloomed.

Two weathered benches were arranged so as to use the shade of the overhanging roof and yet be close to the garden.

They were all rising as I approached. Mrs. Zanger said, "This is Mr. Benbow," and she drifted back into the house.

The captain shook my hand like an old friend and introduced me to his fifteen-year-old daughter, Margaret; his son, Ogden Jr., a boy of seventeen or eighteen; and a stocky, sandy-haired priest named Patrick Salinski. He was dressed in a black suit, his white collar reversed, and he wore high-heeled, thick-soled boots to make himself look taller.

After the introductions I sat down at the end of a bench next to Father Salinski so that I was facing the captain, flanked on either side by his children.

In a moment Rose Zanger brought me a glass of red wine and refilled the captain's and the priest's from a pressed glass decanter.

As the captain continued with his rambling narrative I looked at the three of them and wondered if they were posing for some sort of family tableau. The girl, Margaret, had some of her father's controlled vitality, but it was covered with a soft layer of baby fat that made her look pudgy. Likely if she ever got mixed up in some outdoors activities she might slim down like her mother, but for now she looked like a pussycat in a bawdy house.

Ogden Jr. was modeled after his father, being tall and muscular with the same stiff neck. There was a look of smug self-satisfaction on his face, as if he'd already gone out, conquered the world in his spare time, and retired to enjoy his pension. The youngster's face seemed to dissolve into another with long yellow hair splayed out around it and a bubble of blood rising on its pale lips. *'You old bastard!'*

At the moment Junior seemed to be trying to build up his jaw muscles, flexing his hairless cheeks and twisting his lower jaw back and forth as his father continued with his discourse.

". . . take the case of the one they call No-baño. I saw that half of his cornfield was dry and wasted.

" 'Why don't you irrigate it?' I asked.

" 'Oh, *señor!*' " The captain tried to imitate an earnest Mexican farmer. " 'It is a dry year. If we take all the water from the river, where will the fish live?' Imagine!"

The captain made a superior smile; the daughter and son imitated the supercilious expression.

"Yes," the priest said, "they have no sense of practical affairs. When the daughters reach their fifteenth birthdays they must have a fiesta for the whole village. I tell the parents, 'No, bring your daughter to communion and put the fiesta money into the

124

church building fund,' but no, it doesn't work that way."

Father Salinski shook his head sadly. "Take the case of Laurentino Cervantes. He has five daughters. Last year the eldest had her fifteenth birthday, and Laurentino invited the whole town to a party that ran for four days. Tequila, pulque, aguardiente, mescal, wine, and beer for the grownups, lemonade and jamaica for the youngsters. Everyone had to have a new dress or a new suit of clothes. With that one *Quinze Años* party Laurentino Cervantes spent his life savings. Now they are all working day and night to make enough money for the *Quinze Años* of the next daughter. All spent on frivolity, nothing for the church."

"Where do you come from, Father?" I asked.

"Chicago. And I wish I'd never left," he said grimly.

"Can you request a transfer?" the captain asked.

"The only way I can get out of this hole and move up the ladder, so to speak, is to prove my worth to my superiors," the priest grumbled. "That's the idea behind the new church. If I can raise a nice new building with arches and domes and a big bell, they'll put me in a richer parish, but these people

125

have no sense of the beauty of architecture, nor pride in their faith. They'd rather fritter away their resources on fandangos and witch doctors than show the world how much they value their religion."

"I admire your patience, padre," the captain said. "Perhaps —"

"Dinner is ready," Rose Zanger said from the doorway.

The captain frowned at the interruption but got to his feet and said, "We can continue our conversation at the table."

We filed inside and took our places as designated by the captain.

The captain sat at the head, the priest to his right, and me to his left. Beside me sat Margaret, and across from her young Zanger Junior took his place. There was no place setting for Mrs. Zanger.

Captain Zanger looked us up and down like he was inspecting troops on parade and smiled as if we'd passed.

"Please pray, Father," he said quietly.

Father Salinski prayed for us, for the prosperity of the community, for help with the new church, and then gave thanks for the dinner we were about to receive. Amen.

Mrs. Zanger brought in a heavy platter with a slab of roast beef on it and put it in front of the captain to carve.

We passed our plates for slices of well-done beef, then passed bowls of mashed potatoes and mashed squash along with a big bowl of brown gravy.

"Won't you sit down and eat with us?" I asked her as she put a plate of butter and a pan of corn bread in front of me.

"She will eat later," the captain said, concentrating on trying to cut the tough beef.

"Have you thought of taking the post I offered you, Mr. Benbow?" he asked.

"I doubt if I can find the time."

"This valley will be filled with fine residences and commercial houses in a few short years. It's all been planned and the preliminary work started."

"How can that benefit me?" I asked, chewing hard at the old cow. I thought that tough a critter ought to have been boiled all night and the meat shredded into *machaca* before we tried to eat it.

"I intend to make my fortune here by buying as much raw land as possible before the boom comes," the captain said.

"I don't understand what could bring a boom to this remote neck of the woods," I said, swallowing the lump of gristle and thinking to hell with it.

"Father Salinski foresees a new church rising from what you call a remote neck of the woods."

"But you said a little earlier the people —"

"It won't come from these" — the captain frowned, trying to think of the nicest word — "farmers. It will come from the Pecos Pacific Railroad."

I began to see what he was driving at.

"They're goin' to come through here?"

"It's not been announced, yet it's all but accomplished. That's why Mr. Sharp and former Senator Slade are already established here."

"What's holding it up, then?" I took some watery potatoes and added the gravy that tasted like slightly charred flour paste.

"Tell him how Father Salinski is helping out," Ogden Jr. said, like it was some kind of a joke that couldn't wait.

"Yes, Father Salinski understands the need for progress here and is counseling the natives to sell the land," Zanger said carefully.

"So the Pecos Pacific will give them a big new church." I nodded. "That sounds like a step in the right direction."

"Father Salinski wants a transfer back to Chicago, that's all he cares about," young Ogden chortled.

"It's for the good of all," Salinski said somberly, patting Ogden on the shoulder.

Yes, indeed. It's for the good of the padre, the banker, the politico, the doctor, the merchant, the land speculator, and the Pecos Pacific Railway, I thought. It just wasn't what the old-time, contented natives wanted.

"Sounds like you've got it all sewed up, captain. I don't see what help I can give."

"It is not quite sewed up," Zanger said. "We don't have the proper deeds yet."

"Can't you advise them to bring in the deeds, Father?" I asked, trying the orange squash with butter and molasses on it.

"The deeds are in what they call the archives, which is only an old wooden box containing the documents that have ac-cumulated since their royal grant," the priest grumbled.

"That's easy." I shrugged. "Tell 'em to bring in the box or spend eternity in Hades."

"Even if I were that cynical, no one seems to know where it is, unfortunately."

"Why not just take the land, then?" Junior piped up. "If they don't have the papers, they don't have the land."

"It may well come to that, son. But the problem is that once in a while a self-styled do-gooder like that Marcus Webb turns up and sneaks the matter into the courts. Then, if they produce the documents, we risk losing."

"And they'd be pretty mad at the newcomers, too," I said. "No, it's better to get the documents first — then they wouldn't have a leg to stand on."

"You have a perfect grasp of the situation, Mr. Benbow." The priest nodded. "I can see you are a practical man with a brilliant future here."

"No offense, captain," I asked, "but have you tried to squeeze, so to speak, the information out of them?"

"Only, as you know, with one man named Alfonso Madrigal. It is his land that serves as the center of New Bernardo, although his deed has not yet been discovered."

"We feel that we can achieve more through Christian fellowship than force," Salinski said heavily. "Of course, I cannot condone physical torture."

"You could cut off their marriage rites, Father." Margaret giggled. "That'd fix 'em."

"It's no joke, Margaret," the captain said sternly. "The Pecos Pacific won't commence building up from El Paso until we get this settled."

"They need to use the pass through the mountains?" I asked.

"Not the pass so much as the plentiful water, the established town, and the conjunction of the old trader trails as well," the captain explained. "New Bernardo is an idea whose time has come."

"I say just round 'em up and herd 'em off to the Nations like dirty hostiles," Junior said strongly.

"I'd rather it went through proper legal channels. I don't think we can afford another Marcus Webb." The captain frowned and sawed away at the beef again.

I cleaned my plate with a piece of corn bread that tasted like soap, and as Mrs. Zanger silently took my plate and floated away toward the kitchen Father Salinski lighted up a cigar.

I felt Margaret's knee come up against my leg, and I shifted over a bit. There it was again, and not by accident.

I glanced sidewise at her plump face and noticed she'd half closed her eyes as she cocked her head and looked at me.

Lifting my eyes heavenward, I wondered what the hell did she want. Surely not — not old broke-down, stove-in, short-of-breath Sam Benbow!

I still had a dream of a sweet, demure little wife with a few little cubs crawling around the cabin, but now I began to have some doubts.

"You're old enough to settle down, Mr. Benbow," the captain said. "If you play your cards right, you can be a wealthy man with a fine, upstanding family right here in New Bernardo."

"I haven't seen any single lady candidates yet." I smiled.

"Of course, you haven't met Miss Emily Sharp, the banker's daughter, yet."

"She's old," Margaret snapped, "and she's got warts."

"My dear, count your blessings," the captain said sharply. "The fact is, she has other attractions that make up for her unfortunate . . . ah . . . limitations."

"Being old Sharp's only daughter is some attraction," Junior said.

I felt Margaret's left hand rest on my thigh, and I moved my chair back and said, "I know it's impolite to hurry off so soon after such a delicious dinner, but I promised my partner I'd come right back and see to his condition."

"When may I expect an answer, Mr. Benbow?" the captain asked flatly, irritated that I was running off.

"Depends on Skofer. If he catches pneumonia or something, then I'd have my hands full," I stammered, feeling like a fool coward running away from a fifteen-year-old girl.

As I said good-bye to the rest of them Margaret stood up and said, "I'll see you to the door, Mr. Benbow."

"It's just right there —" I moved quickly, but she beat me to it.

"It's been a pleasure, Mr. Benbow," she said, looking up at me slit-eyed and slowly licking her upper lip. "I hope you'll return soon for more . . . conversation."

"Yes'm," I mumbled, thinking she looked like a pink-nosed possum squinting against daylight.

"Bye-bye . . ." she murmured sultrily.

Benbow, old timer, you need a drink to clear up your head, I said to myself as I walked down the street.

The Lone Star's open doorway beckoned to me, and I strolled inside. "Brandy," I said to the bartender, "the good stuff."

He poured me a glass from an unlabeled bottle, and I sniffed at it first. Made out of grapes, anyway.

Doc Daud stood next to me, but he'd seen me first and turned his larded back on me, blocking my view.

There was no one to my right until the tall cattleman Tom Durham bowlegged over like he was walking on stilts.

"Still determined to go to California?" he asked politely as the bartender poured him a glass of brown whiskey.

"Soon as my partner can travel," I replied.

"I can't keep operatin' much longer," he said mournfully. "These Mexes are rustlin' me blind. Won't be long it's goin' to be them or me and no one in between."

"How do you mean?"

"I mean I'm goin' to call on the Texas Rangers to protect my property by stringin' up a few rustlers as an example," he grated out. "I got my rights, too."

"Whereabouts is your spread, Mr. Durham?"

"It's all open range," he replied. "My cattle are on south, downriver. That's where I'm stakin' out my headquarters."

"How many hands you got workin' the herd?" I asked.

"There's only four, and none of 'em has good cow sense. They mostly just understand Samuel Colt's business."

"I wouldn't be any better. I don't know a cow from a spotted pig."

"You could learn," he said sourly, like I'd insulted him.

"No. I always been slow," I said, finishing up my brandy.

I looked in on Skofer and heard his long snore and the peanut whistle exhalation, and figured sleep was what he needed most.

I wondered what was bothering me about tall Tom Durham. Cracked bell. Didn't ring right. For one thing, he was spending more time in the Lone Star than he was keeping track of his cattle, complaining about not having any hands when he wasn't doing much work himself.

I took my steel dust out of the livery and rode through Old Town, which was slumbering through its after-dinner siesta, and I angled across to the great sandstone cliff. The lane passed through a couple of fields and, at the cliff, turned south. A wedge of broken sandstone talus rose from the path to the cliffside, rockfalls old enough for junipers to sprout and grow in. I went on, looking for the cross that Lupe'd planted.

I found a small pile of red rocks that seemed to have fallen recently, but no cross.

Dismounted, I looked over the area closely but found nothing except a few old hand-cart tracks. I made a wider circle that included the brush growing close to the cliff, and halfway around I found it.

The small cross was made of two pieces of milled lumber laced together with raw-hide. It had been shoved under a clump of

135

greasewood, and if it hadn't been painted pink, I wouldn't have seen it.

I looked down at the pathway where the steel dust was ground-tied near the new rockfall.

Easy to figure that someone had come along, jerked out the cross, and hid it.

But why?

Why bother with getting rid of something so innocuous and so remote?

The Rangers were mean enough, but they were too lazy to go to the trouble.

The native people would be too superstitious to tamper with what might be regarded as a sacred relic.

Yet someone in this valley was bitter enough to go out of his or her way to commit sacrilege. If Zanger was telling the truth, someone had hated Alfonso so much he'd met the battered man after Krimpke threw him out, killed him, then maybe hauled him in a pushcart out here and arranged an accident. Krimpke, Bletcher, Mule Teeth, Rafe, Sidney, or Zanger? Santos? Ignacio, Tiburcio, No-baño? Kiko? Anyone?

I propped the pink cross in the pile of broken red rock and rode on south toward a long rocky rise.

Once over that ridge there were no mountains to block the view, and the color of gray-green was so monotonous you forgot the unanswered questions. It was just plain old dull infinite gray-green, and murder didn't change it any.

The river disappeared in a sandy arroyo, went underground, and would only show when the bedrock rose to bring it up in a stone-rimmed pool.

The steel dust, glad to get out of the barn, reached out with pleasure, his head and tail up, his neck bowed like a proud horse.

I thought a moment about Margaret Zanger and decided I preferred a good horse.

If you prefer a horse to two-legged fe-males, Benbow, you're getting to be passing strange, I said to myself. Didn't make a never-mind — if all I had to choose from was Miss Emily Sharp or Miss Margaret Zanger, I'd stick with my horse.

Of course, Lupe was some different. . . . No nonsense about her. Old enough to figure a man didn't want a giggly plaything; she knew he'd want something substantial like a strong haunch and a knowledge of cooking and a ready, honest smile. Sorry, Steeldusty, if I had to pick between you and her, you'd go back in the barn.

I studied the brands on a few longhorns standing in the shade of a mesquite thicket, and they looked to be all young stock fresh branded with the Bar D, Tom Durham's mark.

Coming over a low rise, I saw on below a patch of willows on the riverbank a rundown cabin and a pole corral. Likely that was the Bar D headquarters. There was no one around, and the only things moving were a couple cow ponies in the corral.

It didn't look inviting. I made a detour around the place in case somebody in the cabin wanted company.

Farther on down, the river came up stronger and showed some movement down the channel until it made a bend through some rocky ledges, and as I rode the steel dust over the old trail I came out with another long view to the south.

A grove of cottonwoods, tamarisks, and hickories grew down there in a little punch bowl, and in their shade was an ancient adobe ranch house.

Riding closer, I saw that it had been built in a square with small rifle ports for windows and a large open area in the center.

The roof was adobe so that it was almost fireproof, and if there was a well inside the patio, the people who lived there could hold off an army of Comanches for a year.

I didn't even hear a rooster crow or a

138

horse nicker. It seemed like it must've been a Spanish fort that was no longer needed, and the people who had built it had gone their own ways years before.

Staying with the trail that ran directly toward what looked to be the front of the building, I saw that the yard was littered with leaves, and a pair of line-backed wild burros stood rubbing their shoulders against a broken-down hitch rail.

I stood in the stirrups, yelled hello at the house, and sat back on the saddle, thinking the place looked so decayed and gloomy it'd be better to turn around and go back to town.

A movement at one of the slit windows caught my eye, and as the octagonal rifle barrel poked out and pointed at me I lifted my hands and yelled, "Don't shoot, I don't want nothing!"

Jamming my stirrups forward, I sent the steel dust to backing up in a straight line.

"Who you?"

"Name's Benbow. I'm just travelin' through," I yelled back.

"What you want?"

The voice was old, feeble, and Mexican.

"Nothing. Water my horse, that's all. I don't mean to worry you none."

"Come in," came the tremulous voice, and

the rifle barrel lowered.

Tying the steel dust to a post, I walked through the windrow of yellow leaves to the oak plank front door and waited. I studied the flint points imbedded in the oak planks, left there as souvenirs.

I heard a shuffling inside, then the door opened.

A gnome of a brown-faced man looked up at me with curiosity on his lined features.

"I don't know you, do I?" he quavered, extending his small, knotted hand.

I took the arthritic fingers gently and said, "No, sir, I'm a stranger, but I mean you no harm."

"Come in, come in," he said, closing the door behind me.

He led me back through a dusty, cob-webbed, unused living room to the kitchen that fronted on the open courtyard. As I expected, there was an aboveground stone cistern and a well with a windlass frame over it. There was room for a few chickens and goats and pigs if they were needed to withstand a long siege.

"It's very old, isn't it?" I asked in a voice I usually reserve for a library or graveyard.

"Yes, yes, very old. Nobody knows. Many generations of my family."

"It's big enough for several families."

"Yes, almost a *pueblo*." He cracked a little smile on his wizened face.

His long hair was pure white, and he was clean shaven. His left thumb was missing, but he still had most of his teeth.

"Do you live here alone?" I asked carefully.

"No. An old woman cooks. But women don't like to be alone here."

"Are you the last of the family?"

"I am Fortunato Contreras Ruiz Valerin, yes, maybe the last. My grandson and an old *vaquero* went out one day, and they don't come back."

"When was that?"

"Maybe two months. A long time. I think that *Norteamericano* kill them."

"Which one would that be?"

"They got a brand like Bar D. They been branding my cattle. I don't let them in here."

"Can you get help from San Bernardo?" I asked.

"How? They don't know. I can't ride no more. *Asi es. Ni modo.*" He shrugged his thin shoulders. "I cannot feed you. I can do nothing."

"This Bar D bunch — did they bring a herd of cattle up from the east?"

"My grandson, he tells me four men are branding our cattle, living in our old line

141

shack up north. They don't bring nothing but a branding iron and guns."

"It happens that keeping brands straight is my business."

"You are too late. Everything is gone except my life, and I have eighty-seven years of age."

"You don't want justice?"

"What good is justice to a falling leaf? No. I only wish for revenge for my grandson and my *vaquero.*"

"Revenge isn't my business."

"I would give a man like you this whole rancho, all of it, if you will bring me the head of the man who killed my grandson."

"You know I can't do that."

"I know." He nodded. "Nobody can do that except a Contreras Ruiz Valerin, and there are none of us left to do it."

"I can see that honest men are sent out here to return the cattle to you."

"What are cattle? They are only wild animals. My grandson was a strong young man." A tear from each rheumy eye slowly made its downward course through the wrinkled map of his face.

# 7

When I returned to the Windsor Hotel I found Skofer in the parlor lying on a horsehide settee with his back propped up on a bunch of pillows. Mrs. Kapp had placed a low marble-topped walnut table with turned legs close to his right hand, and when I came in she was carrying a tray of lemon snaps and a stemmed wineglass containing a pale greenish-colored refreshment.

He had a linen napkin tucked under his ratty little fringe of gray beard and a wan look in his washed-out eyes.

"You're looking better," I said. "How's the bellyache?"

"It's his leg," Mrs. Kapp said. "You can't hurry healing. Not unless you want to risk permanent rheumatism."

"That bad?"

"She's a homeopathic healer," Skofer said in a small, unsteady voice. "We're lucky to have her close by."

"My late husband, rest his soul, was a hurrying man. Twisted his knee once but couldn't wait to hurry on to something else."

She didn't finish. She looked at Skofer like he should fill in the empty space.

"What happened?" he asked dutifully.

"Broke the tendon, and he dragged that leg the rest of his miserable life. That's what his hurry-up got him."

Again she looked at Skofer like a third-grade teacher.

"Not me," he responded correctly; then, with a stroke of genius that promised he'd rise to the head of the class, he added, "Especially when someone as kind as you are, Ada, is close by."

"Drink your tonic, Skofey." She smiled and patted his shoulder.

Skofey! I looked at him closely and saw nothing but guile in his sly blue eyes and the trace of a crafty smile tugging at the corner of his mouth.

He lifted the glass and murmured, "Your health," drank down half of it, closed his eyes a moment, then said, "Ambrosia, my dear."

"What is it?"

"Rhubarb wine. It clarifies the blood and gristles up the tendons," Mrs. Kapp said.

"Would you care for a glass?"

"No, thank you, ma'am," I said, "my blood is easy to spook, and I'm already gristled up pretty good. When do you think the poor old feller can travel?"

"It depends on his rate of recovery," she said, like I had just failed the test and was going back down to second grade.

"I reckon I could have figured that out if I'd thought about it a while," I said. "I guess he can't go to the funeral, then."

"What funeral would that be?" Skofer asked weakly.

"Those two Mexicans and that rabble-rousing jailbreaker, likely," Mrs. Kapp said. "No, I don't think Skofey needs to endanger his health for lowlifes like that."

"Not unless you think you need a man to help out," Skofey said quietly to me, a question in his eyes.

"Reckon not," I said. "You might lose both your legs, and then we'd have to call you Shorty."

"Finish your tonic, Skofey," she said, "then you can have a lemon snap."

I drifted on down the street to the boxy little church and found it was so crowded people were standing out in the street. I was the only gringo attending the service, and I saw no welcome in the faces of the mourners for Joaquin and Timoteo, and yet I believed somebody with light skin and blue eyes ought to stand up for Marcus Webb, if only to show that the issue wasn't brown and white, it was more like right and wrong.

I wasn't there to show my grief, I was there to show my respect.

Let Marta weep her heart out for a dream broken forever — such was the mysterious cure — but for me, I didn't want to be marked as "one of them."

I don't like to be included in any group because I have no alliances. All I have is a job. The boss tells me to look into *Omnia vincit veritas* and get it fixed, that's what Sam's group does. It's a group of one and a half, counting Skofer, and it fixes what the boss says fix.

I had my doubts about Marcus Webb's methods, but they were his. Maybe they were the only methods there were to stop the gutting of San Bernardo. My own opinion was that he should have organized his backing better and waited for us to help him, but then again, maybe the Bernardeños were right: Things happen, and the course of events can't be changed, so you shrug your shoulders and say *ni modo*.

I heard Father Salinski chanting inside and smelled the aromatic smoke of his censer. I heard a little bell tinkle once in a while and the Latin words droning over backshot bodies in boxes.

*Vincit omnia veritas* . . . truth conquers all . . .

I'd come no closer to finding the meaning of *el punto.* Where was the point? Was it a point of land? A mountain peak? A hole in the ground? A grave?

There was silence inside the church, but in about half a minute I heard Father Salinski commence an extra sermon.

"Dear friends and family of the deceased, on this sad occasion I would like to take the opportunity to say that these men perished because they lacked complete understanding. The newcomers have promised us a grand new church if we will only welcome them to the valley and help them bring a new and better life for everyone here. We need not resort to violent acts to oppose their coming. Our Blessed Savior said unto us, 'Turn the other cheek, walk the extra mile, and love thy neighbor.'

"The problem centers on the archives that someone has hidden away, and I say unto that person, Please bring the archives to me, and I will guard them with my life, but I will also speak to the newcomers and show them we have proof of our titles, and in that

147

way San Bernardo shall have the finest place of worship in the whole southwest. Amen."

There was no sound of agreement or disagreement, and there was no music. Later on, if the padre could make a deal with the railroad, maybe they'd have a pipe organ tall as a pine tree that could be heard clear down to Fortunato Contreras's ranch house on a good burying day with the wind right.

There was a movement of the people in the street as they cleared away from the church doorway, and I moved off as the pallbearers, wearing clean white cotton pants and blouses, carried the three coffins out of the church single file. Once in the street they turned left and trudged off toward the graveyard.

Suddenly fifty mounted Rangers in two columns came riding in from the right. Fully armed, but saying nothing, they were a massive force that announced itself as something to fear, if not respect.

Captain Zanger led the file on the right side of the pallbearers and mourners while Sergeant Krimpke led the file on the left.

They rode loose in the saddle, and there were no bugle calls or shouted commands, but it was unmistakably a military force that came not to mourn or honor the dead but to intimidate the living.

I admired the smooth, professional perfor-
mance of the troopers doing exactly what
they wanted to do and showing everyone
they could do it any time there was a threat
to their methods of law enforcement. It was
the iron hand without the velvet glove.

I gave Zanger credit for putting them on
horseback. The appearance of indomitable
force was made doubly clear by simply
elevating the Rangers above anyone else.

They'd have looked like nothing more
than mortal men, grub liners, meat hunters,
goat ropers, culls, and scrubs on the ground
alongside everyone else.

I noticed young Ogden Zanger Jr. riding
close to his father, but instead of keeping
his eyes forward he was grinning smugly
and trying to look fierce at the same time.

I wondered where little sister Margaret
was. Probably making faces at a mirror
through slit eyes and long eyelashes.

I saw Lupe and Marta come out of the
church, staying close to a coffin carried by
Santos and Kiko and four others.

The women were dressed in black with
black *rebosas* over their heads, and they
kept their eyes on the ground as they walked
along.

I followed with the straggling older people

who were being helped by respectful younger members of their families. It wasn't easy for them because the procession climbed uphill to the cemetery.

Fenced with rails and pickets, the graveyard was a riot of pastel colors. The headboards were painted any soft color available, and on some of them hung colored paper chains or different shapes of woven straw painted bright colors and made into ornaments. Over many of the graves were tiny stone houses, doll houses, miniature chapels, painted blue, pink, white, purple, yellow, orange, or green; it didn't seem to make any difference.

Without commands the Rangers on horseback wheeled left and right as the pallbearers passed through the gate. By the time we were all inside the cemetery the Rangers were spaced out at regular intervals and had turned their horses to face inward.

The procession stopped in front of three open graves, and the people gathered around for the final rites.

The tall, long-nosed man wearing a worsted suit, silk shirt, black tie, and polished black boots moved close to the grave, and I recognized him as the schoolteacher, Tiburcio, whom we'd met in Lupe's Café. He wore small spectacles, and his bushy black hair covered his ears. He paused to quiet the murmurs, then called out in a high, clear voice.

"These were our friends!"
"Hail Mary, Mother of God," the group
    responded.
"These were of our families!"
"Hail Mary, Mother of God."
"These were our loved ones!"
"Hail Mary, Mother of God."
"These were men fighting for our land!"
"Hail Mary, Mother of God."
"These men are our martyrs!"
"Hail Mary, Mother of God."
"These martyrs sacrificed their lives for
    us!"
"Hail Mary, Mother of God!"

The responses grew stronger, sharper, and harder as the schoolteacher hammered his meaning home.

"These men are of our valley!"
"Hail Mary, Mother of God!"

I noticed the Rangers were wide awake, and Captain Zanger was standing in his stirrups anticipating that the group might turn into a mob.

"These men gave their lives for us!"

"Hail Mary, Mother of God!" came the savage and fierce response, the words meaning nothing now, only the cry of fury, the fire of revolt.

"They fought against the white
    oppressors!"
"Hail Mary, Mother of God!"

"What are we waiting for?" Kiko yelled hotly.

Zanger touched his hat brim, and in one motion the Rangers pulled their saddle guns free of their scabbards and rested them across their saddle bows.

Salinski stood aside and seemed to be praying.

I could see the crowd reaching mindless hysteria, nearly ready to charge the troops surrounding them without care for the odds against them. I could see how Zanger could solve his land problem in one volley from his troops. I could see this gaudy cemetery as a slaughter pen if Tiburcio Bernal whipped up the crowd any more.

I didn't know. Maybe they'd tear me to pieces with their bare hands for being an outsider, but I was the only one there who could see both sides of the dispute, and knowing that, I had no choice.

"How much do we care?" the
    schoolteacher yelled.
"Hail Mary, Mother of God!"

The crowd responded, lost in the rhythmic tension that was building to its peak.

"Blood!" Kiko yelled, enraged.

The captain touched his hat, and his troops levered in cartridges and lifted their carbines to their shoulders.

"Yes! We care!" I shouted, and, taking my hat off, I moved up beside Lupe and Marta. "We want to lay them to rest with proper respect! We want to honor these brave men by seeing that their bodies are not thrown about by angry people but are buried according to custom! After that we can talk about our troubles!"

The men in white and the women in black stared at me, shocked by what they'd almost done.

"Who are you to tell us our customs, *pinche gringo?*" Tiburcio Bernal came back angrily. "Get out of here! Let us mourn our dead in our own way!"

"You're forgetting, professor, that one of them is a North American known to me who is as dead as his friends, and for the same reason. Let's bury them decently and leave them in peace!"

"Yes! Yes!" Salinski stepped forward and swung his censer over the coffins, then nodded to the pallbearers, who looped ropes under the coffins and lowered them into their graves.

The padre picked up a handful of dirt, scattered it into the holes, and intoned, "Ashes to ashes, dust to dust, we commend these souls unto the loving arms of our Holy Mother."

The women wept, the men stood stolid, and the priest started toward the gate, finished.

The captain touched his hat, the troopers lowered their carbines, and I let my breath out.

I thought it was possible that they could kill every man, women, and child on this hill just to simplify the problem of land titles. I thought that unholy bunch of riflemen would do it and think they should all get medals for doing their duty so well.

I thought maybe I'd saved some lives for a change and maybe made up a little for the blond boy who'd called me an old bastard with his last breath.

*Vincit omnia veritas . . . el punto . . .* Was it

one of these pointed little chapels over someone's grave? Was it this small decorated knoll? Was it clock hands pointing high noon someplace?

The troopers rode back down toward their encampment in a loose fashion, and the people moved back down the hill to the street and went toward Lupe's house, where I guessed there would be a feast for the dead.

I saw tall, bushy-haired Tiburcio Bernal enter Lupe's Café and wondered why he had whipped up the crowd. Why did he hate the newcomers so much? Why had he nearly precipitated a massacre? Did he doubt Captain Zanger's commitment? Courage? Awesome power?

Was he that touched by the deaths of his countrymen that he'd lost his common sense in a fury for revenge?

I followed along with the crowd and saw Father Salinski separate himself and go on toward the church, where he'd likely change from his surplice, put on his regular habit, and go about his business.

I followed along, and no one objected when I entered the café. Obviously the café was too small to hold all the people, so the doors to the patio had been opened, and the mourners were gathered outside under

Lupe's *ramada* or brush arbor, where there were tables made of planks set on crates and covered with dishes the guests had brought.

A bed of mesquite coals under a wire grill served to roast pieces of chicken and thin slices of beef, and to heat the tortillas. Lupe herself was standing by a burly young man who was chopping the skeins of *carne asada* into slivers that would fit inside a rolled-up tortilla. Nearby were onions and tomatoes and peppers chopped up into a fiery salsa. It was simple enough, really. Meat, beans, tortillas, and salsa. Everyone was suddenly hungry, and each helped himself. Young mothers rolled up burritos with deft fingers for the children and for old men and women whose hands were too shaky or stiff in the joints.

On another table were cakes and sweet rolls and cookies, which were wide open for the children to load up on.

No longer was there any sadness or anger. The heated liquid of their emotions had boiled over, and there was nothing left except their normal selves, sweet or sour, however they were.

Lupe left the meat chopper and came toward me. She was not smiling nor showing signs of *bienvenidos*.

"Mr. Benbow," she said grimly.

"Sam, Lupe, please."

"Mr. Benbow, you had no business interfering in our funeral."

"It looked out of control to me."

"You don't understand that we clear our emotions openly and strongly. You *gringos* are all frozen inside, hiding your love and hate and grief. Maybe that's what makes you try to overpower us with force."

"You're talking to good old Sam, not Captain Zanger," I said. "I'm not trying to overpower anybody. I just don't want a bloodbath."

"We were not afraid of the guns!" She tossed her hair proudly. "We don't care anything about their guns. We been here two hundred years, and we will be here another two hundred years."

"Not unless you start using your *cabezas* for something besides *calabasas*." I tried to cool her down some.

"I don't know about you, Sam Benbow. You're not what you say you are. You're not a gringo nor a Mexican. Maybe you don't know yourself who you are or where you're going."

"Can't I just like people or dislike people however they look to me?" I smiled. "Happens I like you and these Bernardeños of yours. That's all that's important."

"There is so much trickery going on ever since the rumors of a railroad coming." She shook her head. "No one knows who to trust anymore."

Tall and strong she was, a powerful, mature woman whose femininity shone in the fine-grained texture of her golden skin, in the flash of her large dark eyes, and in an invisible vitality that seemed to say meet me halfway and we can be creators of our own universe, sensual man and woman coeval.

There was nothing casual about her stature or her way of moving, and her spirit demanded that her man be no less. I thought if a man ever hooked up with her, he'd never come unhooked.

"I'm not selling anything, and I'm not asking for anyone to trust me, either," I said. "Why can't we cut through all this thunder and lightning and just be friends?"

She stared into my eyes, then stepped close and kissed my cheek. "You are a man who has wept real tears for your comrades. I can see that now. You try to look so hard and cold, but I know you are not either of those, even as I'm not afraid to speak this way to you."

I took her wide shoulders, stepped close, and kissed her cheek, then nodded and smiled. "I'm guilty as charged, but don't tell anyone."

"Let me get you something to eat," she said, and I figured that meant we were friends again.

As soon as she went over to the food table the tall, long-nosed, bespectacled school-teacher approached and shook hands, which is as natural to a Mexican as blinking his eyes.

"I want to say hello and tell you my thanks for your speech today," he said in awkward English.

"I was afraid the captain wouldn't understand yours," I said. "Otherwise I would have kept quiet."

"I wasn't thinking." He nodded. "My mind was clouded with grief and anger."

"Can you help me understand the village organization a little better?" I smiled like a dumb *gringo*. "I get so mixed up about who's really the head man."

"It's simple." He nodded and lighted a long cheroot. "There is no head man. The priest heads the religion. Juan Pablo is the water master. I am only a teacher. Lupe speaks for the women. You see, we don't really want a boss."

"Then there are no politics, no police, no taxes?"

"Exactly correct," he said seriously, as if lecturing. "If somebody is drunk and beating a weaker person, Kiko generally hears about it and puts him to sleep. The taxes are our own doing. We work together as a community. If we need to clean out a ditch, we all bring our shovels, even the poor schoolmaster."

While he talked I was trying to understand how this same earnest and charming man could have been that wild-eyed orator up in the graveyard.

"I guess what I'm trying to understand is who keeps the documents of the town."

"The weddings, births, baptisms, and deaths are kept by the priest." He smiled broadly. "That is the way it always is."

"But the public documents, the land grant, and titles of the farms and range outside? Some trusted person must keep and protect them."

"Now I understand. You are asking the same question all *Norteamericanos* ask. Where are *los archivos*?"

"Please understand I don't want to buy them or steal them. I'm just interested in where they're kept safely."

"This is the problem." Tiburcio tapped the palm of his left hand with the index finger of his right hand. "You see, they are

160

such simple people, they don't care about such things. They only know it is their land and that Jaime Reyes owns that farm, and José Galvan owns that piece. So it is too much to worry about where the papers are."

"Then you're saying there are no documents?"

"Oh, no. I just don't know where they are. I've seen them in a very nice wooden box, but it is not a very big box, and a person might have it in a closet or may be using it for babies to sit upon so they can eat at the table, or if the table has a short leg, perhaps someone is using it as a prop."

"Wonderful." I laughed. "I admire your carefree spirit."

"Do you want to see the archives?" he asked.

"Not really." I shrugged. "I think they might be very valuable to someone, though, and when that happens, people steal and kill."

"Not Bernardeños!" he exclaimed. "They never steal and only kill in defense of their honor."

I almost said that he was talking about a new breed of human that hadn't been invented yet, but when they're playing waltz music, as we say, it's better to dance slow.

"Were you educated in Mexico?" I

changed the subject, and he looked disappointed. He wanted to jabber on about some old lady using the archive box for a milking stool.

"It took a great deal of sacrifice, but I finished my education in your St. Louis, because I thought I should be able to teach in English as well as Spanish."

"You're a really dedicated *maestro.* You have my admiration."

"But why not?" he exclaimed again, a faint smile touching his lips. "By the sacred treaty of Guadalupe Hidalgo, which your government signed, we were promised that all schools in lands taken from Mexico must forever have teachers who speak both languages."

"I suppose that clause was written in so that Mexican children would be able to learn in their native language." I nodded.

"Yes, even if they were a conquered people they were promised an education in the language of their parents."

"Maybe in a hundred years the Mexicans will give up their ways and be treated as equals in the United States."

"I do not share this hope with you." Tiburcio Bernal wrinkled his long nose. "Most Mexicans believe their culture is superior to that of the greedy and noisy neighbor to the north. Why should they wish to lower their standards?"

"You're jokin' me now, professor. I'm not too bright, but I'm not a *pendejo.*"

"Yes, we are talking too serious." He nodded, looking down his nose. "The sad time of the day is over. Now it is time to dance and sing, and we will say hello to our dead friends on the Night of the Dead when they come back to have a party with us."

"What does the priest say about that?" I smiled.

"Oh, he says it's proper because it's All Souls Day." The professor laughed, and I realized that he'd been teasing me all along. I thought it would be nice to take the superior, smug son of a bitch down a peg or two.

"Oh, forgive me, my friend!" He put on a concerned look. "You are displeased. You think I'm acting badly, but in truth I want only to lighten up the day."

"Please, professor, no apologies. I have not doubted a word you've said, and I appreciate your educating me in the customs of this beautiful community."

"There you are," came the voice of the lovely Lupe. "I couldn't find you in the crowd."

She handed me a plate with two burritos,

a barbecued chicken breast, and a piece of yellow cake on it. Bernal stepped back and stared at her like a lonely hound dog.

"Bring him a glass of wine, Pico," she said offhandedly.

"You are the perfect hostess, Lupe." Tiburcio Bernal bowed. "Your hospitality is without bounds."

I wondered why he was frowning. Maybe because he was proud and hopelessly in love, and she'd acted like he wasn't even a man.

# 8

Next morning at breakfast in Mrs. Kapp's dining room Skofer looked lazy and fat, sleepy-eyed and half awake, slouching and overfed, stroking his ratty little gray mustache like a preening canary.

"How's the leg?" I asked.

"I can travel."

"Not just yet, please," Mrs. Kapp protested. "You're well on the road to recovery, but we don't want to have complications, do we?"

"Complications?"

"A blood clot or blood poison. You never know."

"Ma'am, Skofer's been through blizzards and hurricanes, a war, stampedes, massacres, and church revival meetings, and he never had a blood clot yet. Why would he start now?"

"Age," she said quickly, on sure ground. "When a person reaches a certain age, it's time to take stock."

"And take to the old rockin' chair." I nodded. "Yes, I seen it coming — the way he's been droolin' out of the corners of his mouth, mistaking salt for pepper, forgetting to button up his pants, mounting his saddle backwards. I reckon you're plumb right."

"What's that?" Skofer sputtered. "Whatever are you obfuscatin' now?"

"Just sayin' you're ready to be turned out to pasture, old hoss, where the wolves will soon gnaw your bones," I murmured sadly. "It happens to the best of us."

"I ain't ready for no pasture, mister," Skofer sputtered. "Just because I got a sprung leg, there ain't nothin' wrong with me!"

"Don't get excited, Skofey, it's bad for your heart. We don't want a thrombosis, do we?"

"Can't button my pants! What kind of man would lie against his own partner? Got a little hitch in my gitalong, nothin' more. Name your poison, mister, I'm ready for you!"

He was up on one foot, hanging onto a chair with his left hand.

"Now see what you've done!" Mrs. Kapp shrieked at me, and she rushed to support his shoulder.

"Me?" I put down my fork and stared at the pair of them. "I'm just passin' the time of day. This poor old-timer has a softening of the brain, I reckon."

"Softenin' of the brain!" Skofer yelped while Mrs. Kapp pounded on his back like she was trying to pump some extra air into him.

"Maybe I heard you wrong, Mrs. Kapp. Somethin' about when a man reaches a certain age . . ."

"That is true," she said. "The graveyard is full of people who didn't take care of themselves in their declining years."

"That's plain enough to me," I said. "Poor feller, you take care of yourself. I don't mind doin' the work of two — it helps to hold back the declining years."

"You see, Skofey? He's not a bit sensitive to your needs," Mrs. Kapp cooed into his ear as she brushed his wispy hair back over his ears like a fixed tabby cat.

I wondered if he was faking a bad knee just to get an extra helpin' of apple pie or whether maybe he was getting a little too old for our kind of work.

Of course, nobody expected him to wrassle the big he-bull of the range, but I figured he could side me some, tell me if somebody was aiming at my back, small things.

Also he was handy for talking to and keeping things straight. Sometimes he could see where I'd gone down the wrong track and was chasing false bait, and sometimes he'd think of a new way to get to the heart of a hard problem.

And God knows I had a hard problem, with everybody wanting the archives, and yet the Bernardeños didn't even care where they were just so they were out of the rain and the mice weren't eating them into lace.

Then there was the old rancher, Fortunato, down at his old hacienda barely hanging on. I figured I ought to do something for him while he was still alive.

And there was Captain Zanger, who seemed to do everything just right and according to the book, yet he was on the greedy side.

There was Marcus Webb, who, dead or alive, couldn't be ignored. It was because of him that we were there. Because of him the archives had become so important. *El punto, ¿Donde? ¿Donde está?*

I wondered what I would do with those documents if I found them. Who could I trust? My choice would be Lupe, but I wasn't sure she could stand up against the power of the newcomers.

Where would the governor stand? Would he side with the new railroad or an old, forgotten village? That wasn't too hard to figure.

Still, I wished I could talk slow, sort of ramble on with old Skofer, without the Widow Kapp interrupting.

I wondered if the village could appeal to the Mexican government for protection against the colonists and their railroad.

Somehow it would take something bigger than the governor of Texas to see the right and do it.

When it came to a new railroad opening up a big country, documents or no documents, the pressure to take over the valley would be overwhelming. The only people who'd be against it were the handful of Bernardeños, most of whom didn't even speak English.

Fat Alfred Slade was the connection between the state government and the railroad, and he was no doubt being paid by both sides.

Why not have a little chat with Fat Alf?

I strolled across the main street of new town and climbed the stairs to the second floor of the bank where Slade had his shingle hanging out:

## Senator Alfred Slade
### *Attorney at Law*

I knew he hadn't been a senator for ten years due to one of his schemes stinking so strong it even puked his colleagues. He'd been advised to retire to private practice, or he'd have been gracing the hallowed halls of Huntsville Prison.

Since then he'd been appointed to various state commissions and worked on the side as a lobbyist, his left hand often paying his right hand. It being the nature of overpaid government office holders to protect one another against all charges of malfeasance, true or false, he had survived and grown wealthier and more powerful as the years went by.

I didn't knock.

A young man in a suit and tie sat at a desk near the front of the long room. The back part was partitioned off so that the ex-senator could hatch his deals in privacy.

"Yes?" the young clerk asked, his eyes skimming over my face and on down to my boots. "You must have the wrong office," he added.

"It says Slade on the shingle."

"But Mr. Slade doesn't take criminal or civil cases." The clerk looked down his nose at me. "Nor does he make out wills or act as a notary public."

"What does he do?" I asked, playing the knot-headed cowboy.

"He draws up contracts mostly, and he advises clients on government procedures."

"That's my man. I need some advice on how to proceed with the government without putting a clothespin on my nose."

"I doubt if you can afford the fee," the clerk sneered, running his hand over his oily hair.

"What is it, Cornelius?" came the heavy, gravelly voice from the back office.

"I really don't know, Senator." The clerk's face reddened as I passed through a little wooden lamb's gate and went on back into the wolf's den.

He sat at the broad golden oak desk like a soft-shelled sea turtle with a broad butt to maintain his balance. His head was completely bald and splotched with brown spots, and it tilted forward on a neck lost in a rumpled bib of pink jowls that disappeared into a wide paper collar secured by a silk string tie. His suit was gray and slick as silk.

On the other hand, you could say he looked like a huge garden toad, liver-spotted and swollen, his beady eyes triggered to his long, greedy tongue.

Whatever else, he did look like an impressive specimen of some kind of creature, one more to be feared than cuddled.

"Benbow," he said. "We met in the Lone Star the other day."

There was nothing wrong with his memory. Chances are he had trained that faculty well because of his fear of written commitments.

"That's me," I said, not offering my hand.

He looked me over closely twice, weighing this against that, pooched out his fat lips, and asked, "What is it?"

"I've been wondering about the missing archives of San Bernardo."

"Why?"

"I suppose a man in your position would like to have them," I said, trying to think of some way to get him talking.

"You're fishing. I don't know why. What is your interest in those papers?"

"Has anybody thought of offering a reward for them?" I got in the key question, and he relaxed, his flabby bulk settling back into his wide oak chair.

"Money. Always it comes to money." He breathed hoarsely through his mouth. "Can you deliver them?"

"If somebody made it worthwhile."

"Do you know where they are, or are you

172

asking for work?"

"I'm asking what would you pay me for the archives if I brought them in."

"The amount would have to be negotiated," he said shortly. "After, not before."

"I'm just shopping around. I might get back to you later."

I turned away and started for the door.

"Wait — sit down. Have a cigar. I'm only trying to be careful in these difficult times." He tried a smile, and if a toad could smile, that's what he'd look like.

I declined the cigar and the chair, but I was ready to listen.

"It is a thorny situation. We cannot find out who is the mayor or leader or *alcalde* — whatever. And we cannot find anyone who is responsible for keeping the records. I would pay you a thousand dollars in gold just to know that much. I would double that amount if you put those records, including the old titles, on my desk."

"Somehow I figured they'd be worth a lot more," I said, sounding disappointed.

"We are running late. You have us, as you say, by the short hairs. There is an opportunity to acquire a great deal of wealth," he said, tired of waiting me out. "Name your figure."

"I figured somewhere upwards of ten

173

thousand dollars would be fair, if you figured the risks involved."

He sucked in his breath, and his eyes bulged. He leaned back in his chair and blew smoke at the ceiling. "When?" he murmured.

"I haven't heard a yes or no."

"How do I know you're not bluffing? I know nothing about you except what you care to say."

"Trying times in a difficult world." I nodded. "It's hard."

"Very well," he said, ruminating aloud, "suppose you brought me those archives and they were all there and bona fide, and there were no copies elsewhere. I would pay the ten thousand in cash."

"That's a number to start with. I reckon the railroad has to have those papers, or they'll find another route west."

"Don't worry about it." He chuckled. "There's more than one way to skin a cat."

"You think of everything," I said, trying to hide my curiosity.

"In my profession it's necessary," he said, opening up under my sudden admiration. "I'll just say that if we don't get those archives very soon, the railroad will pass this valley by, and it will become only a relic of history, unknown to the world and forgotten."

"Then you are not under any pressure to come through here?"

"None at all," he said blandly. "I have not invested a dime in this town yet."

I thought he'd enjoy seeing the other early birds trying to find buyers for their buildings and scuttling off to the new railroad hub, where he'd already be waiting to sell them town lots.

"I'll look around for those archives," I said.

"Take your time, Mr. Benbow." He guffawed and shook all over like a gut bag full of buttermilk.

Down on the boardwalk I wondered if Slade was putting up a smokescreen or not. He'd pay ten thousand in gold for the archives, and out of that deal he could slip out the choicest land before selling the rest to the newcomers and the Pecos Pacific.

It wouldn't matter how they cut it up because the Bernardeños would get none of it.

I thought about myself, my zero bank account, my zero land holdings, my mind going soft at a certain age, my bones creaky, the world changing so fast I couldn't keep up. I wondered if ten thousand would buy us a little ranch in California. Somewhere around San Juan Bautista where Doña Encarnación said it never snowed and the grass was belly deep and there were no Indians or rustlers to fight.

A handful of Confederate medals, that was the net worth of Sam Benbow, unless you counted his horse and his guns. Cow savvy. Got plenty of that. Gun savvy, too.

Sam, quit teasin' yourself, I thought. You ain't never goin' to turn those documents over to Slade, even if you could find 'em. So just settle down and grow old, as they say, gracefully. 'Course, they don't say how to do that when you ain't even makin' wages.

Look at it this way: Maybe somewhere back east you've got a rich uncle you don't know anything about, and when he's ready he's going to leave you plenty enough to take care of growing old gracefully.

I walked across the street, passed by the captain's converted town hall, and went on down to the livery stable.

I found a brush in an old powder box and brushed down the steel dust so he looked like polished gunmetal. He was restless, wanting to get out and run, but I wasn't ready. I stole a quart of oats and put it in his feed box to keep him happy, and I was heading for the open door when I saw the chubby figure of Margaret Zanger standing there waiting.

Seeing me, she came trotting forward, a happy smile on her round face, both hands extended and her arms open wide.

As much as I wanted to, it wasn't in me to cut and run.

In a second she had wrapped her arms around my waist and jammed the side of her head against my chest. She hugged me tight, then stepped back with a little smile and said, "Surprised?"

"Yes, child." I nodded. "Why aren't you in school?"

"Silly," she giggled, "there isn't any school, and besides, it's summertime."

She stepped back and did a twirl, holding her arms up, and said, "How do you like my new outfit?"

She wore short riding boots, a divided skirt, and a new cotton blouse with a pink scarf, and her young body would have looked fresh and fetching if I hadn't known my age and what a devil I had under control most of the time down in my pants.

"Mighty pretty," I said.

"Oh, you big, silent cowboy," she said, laughing, and she made a running jump at me so her arms went around my neck, her legs went around my waist, and her mouth landed smack on mine.

It was the soft, moist mouth that sent a shot of lightning down my backbone.

I was staggered backward by her rush, and I grabbed helplessly at something and ended up clutching at her chubby little bottom.

Still off balance, stumbling backward, I fell back in an empty stall a foot deep in loose hay.

She didn't let go when I fell. Instead she moved her head back and looked me in the eyes with a searching gaze, and then she moved her legs back so she was lying on top of me.

This time she kissed me softer and longer.

I was rattled and confused. It wasn't in me to bounce her against a plank wall, nor hurt her feelings either. I just couldn't understand what this young girl was trying to do to me. I mean, I knew what she was trying to do to me — and she was doing a good job of it, too — but I couldn't understand why.

I tried to relax and hold back, but she was persistent and was running her hands up and down, from my chest to my tailbone, and for one desperate moment I thought, Sam, all you have to do is roll over and rise and shine in the open gates; but then maybe old age grabbed me by the scruff of the neck and gave me a shake and said, You're goin' to end up cat meat. . . .

I pried my hands loose from her pretty little seater and got my right arm between my chest and hers as delicately as possible, although I confess I will never forget the feel of her soft breasts and hard little nipples, and then gently but firmly I pushed her away.

She lay on her back in the soft, sweet-smelling hay, her young breasts rising and falling, her legs spread wide, and her eyes on mine with a look I would have called entreating.

I set my jaw and climbed to my feet.

She looked at my crotch and giggled at what she'd done all by herself.

I turned away in embarrassment.

"Sweetheart," she called softly, "come to me."

"Margaret, you go home and play with your dolls."

"I'm a woman," she said languidly. "Don't you think I'm attractive?"

"I've got to curry my horse," I said quickly, wondering what had gotten into her.

As I moved toward the open door the two young troopers, Rafe and Mule Teeth, walked in. They had a foxy, hungry look on their peach-fuzz faces, and I began to understand maybe what had gotten into her.

"Hold it, cowboy!" Rafe snapped. "What you doin' with the captain's daughter?"

I'd heard stories about army girls who'd went wild because there was so much manhood around and very little female. Sometimes it was a wife, sometimes it was a daughter, but it always went the same way. The female in question, no matter her age, would feel neglected by her husband or father and work a wicked, horrible, insane joke on him by setting herself the goal of seducing every man in his command.

The stories never went much beyond a couple of companies, which at full strength would make it a hundred and fifty men.

Margaret Zanger had a very serious problem in her head, and she had connived with this pair to cut me down for avoiding her at the dinner table.

It was her problem I had to settle first, because she could get a man staked out on an anthill with that innocent baby face and sweet, demure smile.

"Girl" — I turned toward her — "I want to know you better when you're a year or two older. I think we could be pretty good friends."

"Why wait?" she asked, surprised by my straight-out speech and friendliness.

"Because, take my word for it, it'll be better then."

"You never answered me, cowboy," Rafe snapped, cutting me off.

"Wait, Rafe," she said. "Let him finish."

"He's finished, all right," Mule Teeth said heavily, sidling away from Rafe, his hand poised over the butt of his six-gun.

"Boys, it'd be crazy to fight this way," I said, almost pleading. "Hold off and think a second —"

"We caught you in the hay with the captain's daughter," Rafe said.

"And we don't allow that," Mule Teeth said off to the side.

"Margaret," I said, "get out the side door. I don't want you to get hurt."

"You're the one's goin' to be hurt." Mule Teeth tried to laugh, but his voice cracked.

Margaret scampered off to the side and ran out the open door.

"Now then, boys," I said, "you saw she's come to no harm, and you know as well as I do what's goin' on amongst her and you troopers. Don't you think it'd be unreasonable to get yourself killed now?"

"I bet Rafe I get you before he does." Mule Teeth forced a smile, and before I could speak again he yelled, "Draw!"

I palmed the familiar Colt .44, figured Mule Teeth would be quickest because he'd called it, and put my 130-grain slug in the middle of his chest just as he cleared leather. I didn't waste any more time worrying about him but was already making my pivot when I saw Rafe coming up a second faster than I'd expected.

Been practicing, I thought as I fired and saw his .44 belch flame and smoke and felt the whole world spin around.

I didn't know if I'd hit Rafe or not, but there wasn't a second shot from him, and as I gyrated around on one leg the force of the bullet threw me back against the planks of a stall headfirst.

I still held my Colt and made myself turn and look at Rafe even as my knees gave out, and I clung to a plank with my left hand.

He was down, sprawled out in loose angles that became grotesque because we normally never sprawl out that way.

Damn. Damn. Damn. Two more to haunt my nights and dog my days, two more foolish, wrongheaded kids who wouldn't take no for an answer . . .

Then I felt the liquid fire eating into my left side. I holstered the .44 and put my hand where the shirt was ripped and the blood running.

At the same time I found strength to get to my feet and lean back against the stall, trying to think. The Rangers catch me like this, they're not goin' to ask any questions, I figured; they're just goin' to hang me from the haytree.

Got to go. Get out.

No time to saddle up.

I staggered off toward the side door that backed up on Old Town. Margaret had gone out that way but turned and scooted for home.

They'd surely look for me at the Widow Kapp's.

I heard men yelling from the street, and I moved off to my left and stayed close to the adobes with their doors closed on the empty street.

Holding my side, I crabbed down the street until I came to Lupe's Café. Should I try it or not?

Would they hand over a *gringo* to other *gringos* just to watch the fun? Why not?

Would Lupe's door open? Would she let me in?

Pain and questions, aching fire and doubts, confused thoughts rattled by the shock of the wound and the killing of two fool kids.

I stopped a second and thought maybe if I could sneak into somebody's shed or find some brush — anything — it would be better than laying such a risk on Lupe's doorstep.

I heard a chorus of howls as they found the two dead boys. I had only a few seconds, but I was petrified by indecision. I was locked up tight. I teetered back and forth from one leg to the other.

Suddenly Lupe's door opened, and tall, strong Lupe Madrigal came running. She was barefoot and only half dressed, but she wasn't worrying about appearances.

She grabbed me around the shoulders and snapped, *"Vamanos! Ya pronto!"*

It was dark and cool inside, and as I pitched toward the floor I heard the door slam and the bar fall in place.

# 9

Minutes or hours later I felt the scalding pain in my side erupt, and I instinctively swung my forearm up to cover my responsive outcry. My hand thudded against fine hair and skin, and I heard Lupe's voice murmur, "Steady, Sam! We're nearly finished."

I opened my eyes and saw her leaning over me, saw Santos on the other side, and realized the two of them were holding me down while a small, gaunt-faced old lady worked on my side.

She nodded to herself agreeably, brought a handful of blood-soaked herbs away from the wound, and dropped them into a bucket. "It's bigger than Pico's nose," she muttered in Spanish.

"The bleeding has stopped," Lupe murmured.

Lupe let off the pressure from my shoulder, and Santos stepped back as the old lady placed a pad of white cotton cloth over the gouge and tied it in place with a single length of torn sheeting.

"You are lucky," Lupe said. "The bullet is gone. Hortensia thinks it glanced off the rib."

I recalled the whole incident with Rafe and Mule Teeth, their insolence, their self-confidence that rose to self-destructive arrogance. Dumb kids who'd practiced drawing their six-guns and dry-firing so long, they just had to show somebody how good they were.

I had known how good they were and would have run like a yeller dog if I hadn't believed they'd backshoot me. Once they'd started there was only one part left for me to play, a part I would call self-preservation.

There they lay, grotesquely slating up at the sun. Eighteen years of life and then eternity, the mystery of life never unraveled, hardy even touched.

Sure, they were well started on a path of outlawry that might have brought ruin or death to their victims, but they might have changed their ways. I had been a young hellion myself with a hot, smoking gun, but I'd come to a crossroads where I could say yes or no to murder and plundering, and I'd drawn back and said no, I don't want my life to be that way.

Still, you can't say no when you see the shoulder dip, the hand flash, the blue steel on the rise, young eyes open wide with ferocity and the thrill of mortal combat. If you say no, it's the last time, and when it comes to life or death, I'll take life.

They say that in Mexico on the Night of the Dead the ghosts come swarming out of their graves and make a great chorus, singing, "Live, live, live, live!"

So you do the best you can. You give them nothing once they make their move. Even doing your level best, heart pumping hard, one of them puts a lead slug a whisker off from a fatal wound.

Still . . . their open eyes stating up at the sun . . . their wolfy grins twisted into a fixed rictus of horror . . .

The wizened-up old lady backed away and nodded to Lupe and Santos.

"*¿Los cabrones?*" she murmured, jerking her small chin toward the street.

Lupe put her index finger across her lips and shook her head.

The old lady nodded again, picked up a goatskin bag, and crossed the room to the open back door.

"Are they looking for me?" I had to ask, even though I could guess the answer easy enough.

"Yes," Lupe said quietly. "Soon we must put you up on the roof, but without tearing open the wound."

"The roof?" I frowned, not liking the idea. It sounded more like a trap than a hiding place.

"It is all there is," Santos said. "Can you hold onto the ladder?"

"I'm game."

Kiko scurried in the back door and rattled off something in fast Spanish.

"They're coming!" Lupe said to me urgently.

"Let's go."

With Lupe and Santos on either side I worked my legs and tried to shut out the pain that came with every motion like a searing shadow following along.

Kiko and Santos went up the ladder first, and Lupe helped me get my right boot up on the first rung while my hands gripped a rung above my head.

*"Listo!"* Lupe snapped, and the two men on the roof leaned down and started pulling the ladder and me up through the hole in the ceiling.

As soon as I was started Lupe lifted the bottom of the ladder and pushed hard.

In a second I was stretched out on the

ladder lying on the roof.

Santos, still on his knees, dropped the cover over the hole and crawled back to me with a smile of hellish ferocity on his gaunt face.

A low adobe wall ran around the roof to keep the wind from blowing away the drying chilies, fresh-dug garlic, and tied bunches of herbs and spices. There was even a pile of white corn on the cob stored away from chickens and barnyard animals.

Next to the back wall lay a mattress covered by a blanket, partially shaded by a tall laurel tree in the back patio.

Santos and Kiko made signs that I should move over onto the mattress. I eased myself slowly and silently off the ladder and crawled on hands and knees, with the men on either side making sure I didn't collapse.

The few feet seemed like a journey of a thousand miles. I suppose it was losing so much blood and the letdown from shock that made every muscle movement a massive problem. When I reached the mattress I felt a cover of exhaustion and lassitude coming down over me in spite of the closeness of the troopers.

I heard horses in the street, imperious rapping on doors, harsh voices demanding answers. "Where did he go?"

*"No se."*

"Where is he?"

*"No comprende!"*

"Answer me!"

*"¿Mandé?"*

I heard rapping on Lupe's door and the raspy voice of Griff Bletcher. "Open up!"

"What do you want?"

"I want that big gringo. He's bleeding."

"Look around. He is not here."

"Where's the ladder that goes to the roof?"

"Somebody borrowed it last Christmas and never brought it back."

"Where is he?"

*"No se."*

"Where did he go?"

*"No comprende."*

"Answer me!"

*"¿Mandé?"*

With Lupe Bletcher took longer.

"What are you doin' with that chicken?"

"I remove the guts."

"Why don't you do it outside?"

"Blood makes the floor harder."

"What about flies?"

"What flies? I don't see flies."

"You got a smart mouth, woman. What else you got?"

"There is always a knife for the pig."

"Dare me, you bitch, and I'll be back later."

"Get out of my house!"

"I'll see more of you, *puta!*"

The door slammed shut, and the search continued on up the street.

"My horse?" I muttered to Santos, trying to tell him that when they found my horse in the livery barn they'd know I was close by.

Santos wiggled his index finger at me sidewise and whispered, "We move him."

For a sleepy-looking bunch of lazy Mexicans, they'd been busy, I thought drowsily.

The sounds of the search faded out as the troopers moved on toward the outskirts of the village and a dove started to coo from its nest in the laurel.

I asked Santos, "what does *el punto* mean to you?"

"A point." He shrugged his shoulders. "Why?"

"I'm looking for something. . . ."

I drifted off into a dreamless peace and awakened only when I heard Kiko and Santos moving the ladder.

Staying low, they pushed it over the wall and let it drop down to the patio so that it leaned against the back of the adobe.

"Stay here," Santos said, and he followed

191

Kiko down into the patio where they held a quiet conference with Lupe.

I drifted in and out during the afternoon, sometimes hearing the troopers' horses charging up and down the street, sometimes nothing but a rooster crowing his valor across the valley or the mourning dove's small pealing of its mournful chime.

Toward dark Lupe climbed the outside ladder and brought me an *olla* of water and some fried chicken and tortillas.

She took one quick look at the bandage, murmured, "Good," then hurried back down when someone knocked on the front door.

"I'm coming," she called, and I heard the front door open.

"Lupe Madrigal?"

It was the captain himself.

"That's my name."

"Please come with us."

"Where? Why?" she cried out strongly.

"To headquarters," the captain said stolidly. "We are questioning the prominent people of the village."

"I know nothing. Ask your questions here."

"At headquarters," the captain said. "We don't want to use force. . . ."

■ ■ ■ ■

She hadn't returned as the sun started to set, and I wondered if Zanger was using her for bait to bring me out.

Yet I could think of no way he could know that I had any connection with her. Skofer and I had eaten dinner in her café the first day we were there, and I'd come to the café after the funeral, but no one, not even Lupe, suspected what I felt in my heart.

I doubted if Kiko or Santos would talk, not because they had any loyalty to me, but they seemed strong in their loyalty to Lupe.

Staying near the back wall, I managed to get to my feet and come out of the crouch without tearing anything open in my side. The pain was lessening, but the edges of the gouge prickled and itched.

I looked down into the courtyard and saw that they'd moved the ladder and leaned it into an old apple tree so it looked innocent enough, but it left me stranded on the roof.

Twilight blended into the last golden light of the sun and a hush came over the valley. I decided I'd wait until it was dark, then drop down off the roof. If I didn't break anything, I'd go on the prowl for Lupe.

I thought if they had hurt her in any way,

I'd kill Zanger first, then work right on down to the last private, and to hell with haunted dreams and the immutable gray faces of the dead.

I studied a side branch of the laurel and thought if I could lean out and grab onto it with both hands, it'd bend under my weight and make me a soft landing on the ground, gentle as a butterfly landing in a bed of daisies.

I heard faint footsteps in the street and the front door open.

She was back.

As I breathed a sigh of relief she came out into the courtyard and saw me leaning over the wall.

She pushed at the air with both hands raised, telling me to lie down, then disappeared back into the café.

I knelt back down on the mattress, took off my gun belt and boots, and stretched out. The evening was warm, the adobe walls held the sun's heat, and the twilight yielded to darkness.

Once again I drifted off into my own darkness, and I dreamed I was folding up a soft doeskin shirt with fringes at the shoulders and tiny glass beads sewn into an intricate design around the bottom.

I laid my face against the warm doeskin

and I breathed in a fragrance of fresh-cut lilac blossoms. I snuggled closer to the warmth and wondered at its unyielding softness.

Somewhere a fine line appeared in the depth of the pleasure, and a part of my mind separated and observed the other part's fantasy gradually becoming larger while the other grew smaller, until there was more of me watching the dream change into the reality of my face pressed against a warm female.

Time to sort out the doubts of what was real and what was not.

I slowly passed my hand down her shoulder, across her smooth, opulent breast, down the sensuous curve of her abdomen across to her hip and concluded the lady was pleasantly nude.

I listened to her breath and felt her heart beat against my lips.

I felt her shift and slowly sit up so that she could undo my shirt.

"Does your side hurt?" she whispered, drawing the blanket over both of us.

"Not now," I murmured.

"Don't get any ideas," she said, touching my lips with her finger. "We're not playing, we're sleeping. All right?" Maybe it was all right, maybe it wasn't. My feeling was relief that I no longer felt alone. I felt at that moment that I could insist and enjoy the quick swing off into the starry pool, but that I would lose the honest trust that she now placed in me.

Better to let the breeze decide, let the lilac blossoms decide, let the future decide. For now, rest with her richness close and warm, trusting and sharing the night without greed or fear.

The pain in my side was lost and forgotten, unimportant.

The pain in my chest was not real, it was only the congestion of human man and woman forces coming together there, and I thought this is the woman who cares for you, this is the beginning, this is the other half of you.

Her face rested on my chest, her left arm draped over my legs, and with every breath a bond was forged between us that I thought of as a profound trust, but there are probably other words.

I didn't consider it as love, a high-falutin word that in my life's working had seemed a temporary, flimsy emotional excuse for youngsters to use while exploring the limits of their bodies. That wasn't trust. Even while they were promising eternal devotion they were thinking of how they could tip off their closest friends about how she could do this and he could do that.

I thought there in the starlight that we had enough confidence in our maturity that there would be nothing to say to anyone, even each other.

Her fine, fragrant hair fell across my face as she moved her head, and I felt her breasts against my chest, and I kissed the hollow of her throat.

Slowly, ever so slowly, in drowsy lassitude, her body moved higher, and in time she cupped my head close with her left hand and I tasted the hard nipple mounted on the melon of her breast.

After a long moment she slipped away, and in the sharing came the trust.

Once again she slept on my chest and I drifted on in the diamond-shot sky, the village hushed as a broody hen, the warm night lulled by the soft plateau breeze.

"Oh, my woman," I whispered into her fine, damp hair, and she held me close.

Before even the first pale stroke of dawn limned the eastern horizon she stirred and knelt on the mattress and found a robe draped on the low wall.

I saw her standing as a tall and powerful shadow in the starry night, but before she could leave I touched her thigh and said, "I need to talk."

"Come," she whispered.

I dressed and followed her down the ladder, feeling the sharp teeth gnawing at my side, but not with the aching pain that had only the day before made me weak and sick.

After lighting a lamp and building up the fire in the kitchen she turned to me, her face aglow, happiness in her eyes, and said, "*Querido mio,* what is it?"

"I can't stay up there any longer. Do you know of an old rancher downriver named Fortunato Contreras?"

"Of course, he was the godfather of my father."

"Are there any great-nephews in town, men related to him, strong enough and willing to fight?"

"Kiko is one, and he has two other brothers and a lot of cousins. The answer is yes."

"The old man is nearly finished. He's starving to death down there."

"But he has his grandson, Fortunato."

"He thinks his grandson and another *vaquero* are dead. He and an old lady are holed up in the ranch house while some rustlers are taking their own sweet time stealing his stock."

"I'll find Kiko," she said, going toward the back door.

198

"I'll need my horse, too."

"Please wait until you're stronger," she said, turning back.

"There's no time. Please."

"As you say." She nodded and went out into the first light of dawn.

I didn't know if there was a direct connection between the would-be rancher Durham and the other newcomers, but it hardly seemed an accident that he should arrive in San Bernardo and start his campaign against the Contreras ranch at the same time.

After a few minutes Lupe returned with Kiko. His round face was sleepy, but his eyes were alert when I repeated the story of my visit to the beleaguered ranch.

Even as I spoke other young men moved through the back door and quietly listened. There were four of them, and they all had the same slant eyes and tough, round bodies.

Lupe passed around mugs of coffee and slices of sweet bread.

"Why didn't you tell me yesterday," Kiko hissed at me angrily.

"I was busy yesterday."

"Yes, of course," Kiko said apologetically. "We are going. *Andale.*"

"Wait, Kiko, I want to go along."

199

"We are enough," he said. "You are hurt."

"It's partly my fight, and I can't stay here."

Kiko made a quick decision. "As you say. Your horse is with mine."

"Be careful, *mi vida*," Lupe said as I followed them out.

"You, too. Zanger won't quit."

In the near darkness we filed out of the courtyard into the alley, turned left, then made another left that took us to a pole corral hidden behind a line of black walnut trees.

I found my steel dust saddled and waiting, and the others were ready by the time I tightened my leathers and climbed aboard.

With Kiko leading we walked our horses past the last house to the south of the village as the roosters commenced their crowing contest. Clear of town, Kiko put his pinto into a long trot that would take us the many miles to the ranch without killing the horses.

My carbine was scabbarded under my right leg, my Colt on my hip.

"We see the brand changed, we kill all," Kiko called out once, and those behind him nodded agreeably.

Looking them over, I wondered if they meant to do it with their machetes, the ancient horse pistol Kiko had slung over his

200

saddle horn, or the couple of single-bore fowling pieces in our arsenal.

These men were brave enough to do it with their teeth, but I didn't believe they could even get near the rustlers with six-guns.

We followed the riverbed on southerly, coming to the old line camp a little before noon. We studied it from the rise and decided if there was no smoke in the stove-pipe and no sign of life, there was nothing there for us.

Kiko raised his straw hat, and off we went south again toward the old hacienda.

We saw cattle along the way with doctored brands that ended up being fresh Bar Ds.

Our horses were showing the effects of the long ride, but Kiko never slackened the pace until we heard the distant boom of an old heavy-caliber rifle.

Kiko held up his hat, stopped, and turned his pinto to face us, his round face rigid, his dark eyes keen.

"We don't do nothin' crazy. We try to be smarter. Felipe, you take your brothers around to the back. We'll come at them from the front, but if there's a big bunch, we'll lead them off, and you catch them from the side. *Andale!*"

I stayed with Kiko, admiring him for not

just rushing into a hornet's nest. I hoped he'd live a long time.

We halted on a rocky rise where we could see Durham's crew lined out afoot among the cottonwoods, their horses tied back in a hickory grove.

"Better to take their horses first?" Kiko put it as a question to me.

I nodded and said, "Somebody lean and quick as a snake."

"Ozwaldo!" Kiko spoke sharply. "Sneak in there and lead those horses out. If those *cabrones* see you, just stampede them and get yourself out."

Ozwaldo, swift as an Apache, using the timber for cover, worked as close as he could, then dismounted and snaked through the brush to the horses.

I figured nothing short of a prairie fire could unnerve a cowboy more than finding himself set afoot out there.

I came down off the saddle with my carbine, and Kiko extended his hand toward the Winchester and said, *"Prestame, por favor."*

He was the leader, and I put the carbine in his hands.

Durham, on down the line, noticed the horses moving away and gave out a yell.

The near puncher turned and threw a shot

at Ozwaldo.

Kiko set his sights on the middle of his bulky torso and squeezed off.

The horses, hearing the whine of the shots, stampeded on their own, and Ozwaldo scuttled back through the brush to his mount.

Durham saw us on the rise at the same time Kiko fired again, dropping the man next to Durham. That left him and two other punchers, and he was momentarily paralyzed with fear. Without a horse he couldn't run; without a rifle he was caught between us and the old hacienda.

The big old buffalo rifle boomed from one of the slit windows, and Durham whirled around just as Felipe led his brothers on a charge from back of the hacienda, *ki-yi*-ing like Comanches.

Durham stood his ground and sighted in Felipe while the others made a run for the hickory grove.

Beside me the .44-40 fired, and Durham seemed to break in half, his upper torso slumping down while the stringbean legs still stood erect.

Felipe galloped past the crumpling Durham, swinging his machete, and on either side of him were his crazed brethren.

The running gunsels went down as machetes cleaved, split, hacked, and severed. Felipe's sharp blade came across with such ferocity and power that the head of the second man separated from the neck.

"Is that all?" Felipe called out to Kiko.

"Is enough?" Kiko grinned, handing me back the carbine.

The battle had lasted only a few seconds, not long enough for the new warriors to use up the fire that had been slowly building from fear and anger, and they rode in aimless circles, whacking off the tops of saplings with frustrated ferocity.

"That rifle sure did good!" Kiko said proudly.

"What about old Fortunato?" I asked when they'd cooled off a little.

"Holy Jalisco! I forgot about him!" Felipe smacked his forehead with the palm of his hand.

"Don Fortunato!" Kiko called. "Uncle! Don't shoot no more!"

"*¿Quien está?*" came the querulous croak.

"It's your family, uncle. Felipe and Kiko, Anselmo, Pepe, and Ozwaldo!"

"*Ven!*"

## 10

We rode to the fallen-down hitch rail and
ground-tied the horses. The scarred plank
door opened, and old bent-legged Fortunato stood ready with his Sharps buffalo
rifle, which was taller than he.

"Those *cabrones rateros?*"

"Those coyotes *viven no mas.*" Felipe
smiled and went forward to make his *abrazo*
with the old man — the handshake, the hug,
three pats on the back, the handshake, the
nod. Kiko followed, then the others, all
performing the same ritual of respect for
their old blood.

"Come in," Fortunato said. "We don't
have much to eat —"

"We brought plenty. Please, uncle, rest.
Let us do it. You are looking well. How is
your housekeeper?"

"She's too old to move." Fortunato
grinned. "Sometime, if you think about it,
fetch me out a sixteen-year-old fatter than

205

Pico's nose."

"*Ai ai!* Look out!" The youngsters laughed. "Once the old rick of straw catches on fire, you can't ever put it out!"

When they calmed down old Fortunato asked, "My grandson Fortunato?"

"We have not seen him. We thought everything was all right with you and him and José until Don Sam told us."

"Fortunato is dead somewhere," the old man said bitterly. "That tall *puto* stoled many cattle. Then he wanted this place, the home of the Contreras. I wouldn't let him in, but he thought it would be easy to starve me out. Two hundred Comanches tried to starve my grandfather from this house and could not. That *gringo pendejo* wouldn't listen."

"Easy, old uncle," Ozwaldo said. "We can bring back the cattle, and there are plenty of the family who will help out."

"Did he say why he wanted this place especially?" I asked.

"He said that he would tear all this down and make a new hacienda for travelers," Fortunato murmured weakly. "But I said all we need is a bunch of willing young men to fix up the roof, and this hacienda will last another hundred years."

"You strong young men are going to have

to bury those hombres right soon," I said to them. "I'm riding back to town."

I left them as they heated up their tortillas and beans, and I rode a loop farther south.

Something bothered the back of my mind about Durham's attack on the old house. It was foolish, for one thing, and Durham had looked hard and sharp, a man who had lived by not being foolish.

He and his crew could have stayed up in the line shack another three months before the blue northers started. He could have consolidated his cattle rustling, the new brands would have healed, and he'd have been home free. Yet he'd gotten in a hurry to take over the hacienda. Right then his foolishness caught up with him.

I rode downstream, clear of the thick growth of hickory, black walnut, cottonwood, junipers, and piñon.

Not far from the hacienda I cut an east-west trail that looked as old as the hacienda and was probably the reason for its being there, because just a short ways to the east was the north-south trail that passed through San Bernardo and went on northwest.

I stopped the steel dust at the crossing of the river and let him drink. Even in the middle of the summer there was plenty of water in the river pools. One of the trails came across from Austin and the other from El Paso, and they both showed old wagon-wheel ruts, which meant that one would go northerly toward Denver and the other would go due west toward Santa Fe.

From the look of the clearing and the old rock-ringed fire pits, this crossroad had once been a favored campsite for teamsters.

Why not? There was plenty of water, wood, grass, shelter, and the ground was flat.

I thought if I was going to put a railroad through this country, I'd follow the old trail, and I'd put a station right there.

Of course, San Bernardo Valley had the advantage of people already settled there, a work force in place; but except for that, what difference did it make?

Senator Slade had figured it out. The others hadn't.

Slade would jump either way depending on where the most money was.

Slade wouldn't worry about an old Mexican's life, but he wouldn't snuff it out himself. He'd send somebody else.

What had he said?

"Don't worry about it, mister, there is more than one way to skin a cat."

He would play hell skinning that cat so

long as the old man's nephews and cousins were living there. He wouldn't know it, though. He couldn't know what had happened to Tom Durham and his crew. Only when he sensed some disaster would he ask Captain Zanger to take a detail downriver and see if maybe some Comanches had caught up with the cattlemen.

Zanger would find nothing. The Mexicans would say nothing. Slade and that unholy crew of newcomers would fry in their own grease.

"We are running late," he'd said . . . and that meant the Pecos Pacific wanted to start laying track.

With it pretty well settled in my mind, I turned the steel dust up the northwest trail and let him make his own pace. He knew where we were going as well as I, and he knew how much bottom he had to do it.

Riding along, I wondered why men like Slade and Sharp had to slink around, covertly doing business, unable to work in the open, broad daylight, as if an honest look might hurt the business.

They couldn't just go to the people of San Bernardo and say we'd like to buy some land for a section house and a depot. They had to sneak in, steal, murder, try to subvert a simple government, not for the sake of

America's good, but for the sake of personal hog-minded greed.

Take it easy, I told myself, you're beginning to sound like an out-of-work professor.

My mind crossed over to Professor Tiburcio Bernal. Where did he stand in this covert business? He'd whipped up the people into a near-suicidal charge at the funeral, and yet he'd lectured on peace and moderation a few minutes later. A strange man, but then, I was not acquainted with very many professors.

The sun set in a lurid vermillion glow over the western mountain scarps, and a few white clouds were filled with gold dust that slowly changed to purple as the sun dropped below the horizon.

It was dark when I came into San Bernardo and detoured around the Ranger camp, where Krimpke and Griff Bletcher would be pleased to meet me and pound me down into the ground like a tent stake.

I rode the back alleys until I came to the rear of Lupe's courtyard and stopped under an old pepper tree.

A lamp burned in the café, and I walked quietly across the worn flagstones to the back door.

Through a small windowpane I saw her sitting at a table, her back to the window.

I stepped back into the deeper shadows and made a whippoorwill whistle twice, something that never happens.

In a moment the door opened. She stood in the doorway looking out into the yard. I couldn't see her face in the shadows.

"¿Quien está?"

"Sam." I stepped out, her broad shoulders slumped, and she backed into the room.

I came along quickly, worried at the change in her.

Her long, dark hair hung down, partially hiding her face, and as I came close she moved back into the shadows.

"What is it, Lupe?" I asked quietly.

"A hard day only," she said. "Things sometimes don't go so well as other times."

"No, there's something else. . . ." I persisted and moved her long hair back from the side of her face.

The bruises were there, swollen, dark purple lumps. I pushed back the other side of her hair to see the welt and split skin.

She was looking at the floor, and I took a deep breath to give me time to control my voice.

"Who did this to you, Lupe?"

"A Ranger. The big one. They call him Griff," she murmured. "It is nothing. . . ."

"What else?"

211

"It was strange. Someone told them you were here. They searched and broke many things. When they couldn't find you they thought I knew where you went."

"Who among your people would talk to them?"

"Perhaps someone spoke to the padre."

"Yes . . . *asi es*. So it is. What else?"

"I want you to promise me something." She was still looking at the floor.

"Tell me."

"If I tell you, promise you won't do anything until I've had my chance to do it myself."

"I cannot promise that. Tell me."

"I must have your word first."

"All right." I nodded. "So long as I think you can handle it alone."

"I will handle it alone!" she said coldly. "That big man, Griff — when he hit me with his fist I took out my knife — but the other one — the sergeant — grabbed it away and broke it in two. They both laughed at my fury, then the sergeant winked at the big man and walked outside. The big man, this Griff beast, hit me three times, very hard and fast. I fought back with my fingernails and teeth. He had a ring on his left hand. I fell, and he laughed. He leaned over me and hit me in the back of the head. After that —

I don't remember. . . ."

"It's all right," I murmured, touching her shoulder.

She shuddered at my touch and pulled away.

"He used me badly — very badly — many times — many ways. . . . When I was half awake he was standing over me. He said he'd kill me if I made trouble for him."

"I'll take care of it," I said grimly as white-hot rage tore up through my midriff and torched my mind.

"No, Sam! You promised!"

"He's too big for you."

"Sam! I must destroy that man, or I cannot go on!" Her tone was desperate and pleading.

I made myself keep quiet and had to walk around the room twice before I could speak coherently. "Lupe, there's a pattern in this we can't see right now. I think when we know more you may have your chance."

"I have another knife," she said fiercely, bringing out a long-bladed bowie that had been smithed with care and honed fine. "I will have his *huevos* first."

"I think you should, but that will come in its own time. I think we should speak to Santos."

"Santos has not come in all day." She

shrugged.

"Can you show me his house?"

"Of course. It isn't far," she said hurriedly, glad to have something to do.

She wrapped a black rebozo about her shoulders and led me out the back way to the alley, where she turned right and moved toward New Town. Turning left, we went down a small walk between old lime trees and came to an adobe almost hidden in the forbidding shadows of old trees.

There was no light in the house. Lupe took my arm and whispered, "Except for his old dog he lives alone. He's at a meeting, or he's gone to bed. The dog doesn't bark —"

"I don't like it." I shook my head. "It's too early."

"They could be waiting in there for you," she whispered.

"Stay here," I murmured, and I felt my way around to the back corner of the house.

I waited but heard no movement inside.

I felt along the wall toward the back door, then stumbled over something in the way. I stepped back and waited for some response. Nothing.

Kneeling, I touched a small, long-haired form, cold and stiff. The blood was almost dried. It had been a small, old dog.

The back door was open.

I stepped on in, and the plank floor creaked under my weight.

A faint moan came in answer. I stopped to let my eyes adjust and saw a shadowed form amid a tangle of litter. I eased across the room and knelt and touched cloth, the white cotton of the Bernardeño. My hand found the shock of black hair and touched the mangled features of a man.

I stepped backward and opened the front door. Lupe was there and followed me back to the still-living form.

Lighting a phosphor, I cupped it in my hands and found a votive candle to light.

"Oh, God in Heaven!" Lupe sucked in her breath at the sight of Santos's ruined face. One eye was open and stared blindly. The rest was a grotesque slab of raw meat that showed a bloody slit of a mouth and not much else. Another little moan brought a red bubble to the slit of mouth.

Running my hands over his arms and legs, looking for broken bones, I found plenty of bruises and blisters burned on his hands, but his frame seemed intact.

I took the chance and lifted the slim man in my arms and followed Lupe into the simple bedroom.

She lifted a woolen blanket and I laid him

beneath it.

She slipped off his huaraches and brought the blanket up to his throat.

"Can you talk, Santos?" I asked in a whisper.

There was no response. He was alive, his heart was strong, but he'd taken such a beating he was either unconscious or simply unable to speak.

I doubted if time would ever heal his face back to what it had been.

I noticed that the bedroom had been ransacked, the same as the front room. An old chest of drawers was emptied, the cornshuck mattress split, a board pried from the floor.

Lupe returned with a pan of water and a wet cloth.

She carefully cleaned the deep gouges, and the mottled, bloody mask started to have some shape to it. The jaw wasn't broken, but he'd lost a couple of teeth.

The beating had been slow and deliberate. Someone wanted information about me, or the archives, something important enough to risk the fury of the townspeople.

"It's Lupe and Sam," she whispered as she dabbed at his face. "You're all right now, Santos. Who did this to you?"

He seemed to shake his head.

Probably someone had stunned him in the dark, gagged and blindfolded him, then started the torture.

"It must have been the same men," she muttered darkly to me.

"I don't think so. . . ." I shook my head. "Those aren't ring marks on his face."

"There are too many things we don't know," she said somberly.

"Can you hear me, Santos?" I asked.

His head nodded a fraction of an inch.

"Can't talk?"

Another nod.

"Been hit too much in the mouth and the throat," I said. "Tongue's swelled up. Maybe cracked his voice box."

"Do you know who did this to you?" Lupe asked.

He shook his head no.

"One man?"

A nod yes.

"Mexican?"

No answer.

"*¿Gringo?*"

No answer.

"I'm going for the *curandora,*" Lupe said, putting the bloody cloth in the basin. "I can do no more."

When she'd gone I asked, "Do you know what he wanted?"

Santos nodded.

"Was it about me or Lupe?"

He shook his head.

"About the Rangers?"

No.

"About the newcomers?"

No answer.

"About the archives?"

A nod, yes.

Someone was getting desperate to find the grants and deeds. Someone was pushing for more haste.

Senator Slade.

But this wasn't Slade's work. He was a fat toad in a hole, a bloated smile and a long tongue for picking off gnats and butterflies. So long as Slade thought he had the alternate site, why the hurry?

I felt too tired; my head wouldn't work anymore. It had been too long a day.

No . . . it was someone who wanted the documents for his own use.

I heard the soft shuffle of the huaraches, and the bowed-over old lady came in carrying her bag of salves and herbs.

Lupe was right behind her.

The old doctor studied Santos's face and gently ran her finger from his jawbone down his throat to his collarbone.

"¿Sientes eso?" she asked softly.

A head shake no.

She nodded to herself and turned to Lupe. *"Agua caliente."*

I followed Lupe into the primitive kitchen and said, "There is nothing I can do here. May I sleep on the roof tonight?"

"Pull the ladder up after you — there is a beast, a monster out there."

*"Hasta mañana,"* I said tiredly. I turned and followed the zigzags of the path back to her courtyard.

Lupe's lamp shown through the open door onto the courtyard. The ladder leaned against the wall, and I put my foot on the bottom rung and heard the scrape of a boot behind me. Instinctively I ducked forward.

A crushing blow landed against my hat brim instead of the side of my jaw, and I rolled along with it, turning to face whoever it was.

All thoughts of tiredness were instantly forgotten as well as all expectation of a soft bed under the stars.

It came out of the shadows as a lashing boot aimed at my crotch, a big number twelve that would put me out of commission permanently.

I leaned back, and as it came up level with my belt I bent forward and grabbed the heel and toe with both hands and threw myself sidewise and down, taking the leg on around with me.

In that instant I saw the scarred face of Griff Bletcher, his face dark red with rage, his eyes like razors shining behind his slit eyelids.

He'd come back for another go at Lupe and found me instead.

Fine!

I cut my own wolf loose. I didn't want to fight him, I meant to kill him.

He screamed as I bent his leg, but I hadn't the leverage to break it, and he tore free. I pulled my .44, but he came down with a chop to my wrist that felt like a pick handle, and I lost the gun.

It didn't make any difference. I'd kill him with my bare hands. I'd gouge out his eyes and tear out his tongue. I'd bite off his ears and wring his neck like he was a red rooster.

Suddenly a spinning whirl of lights exploded inside my head, and I felt myself falling.

I'd been so intent on what I meant to do to him I'd forgotten he was not only taller and wider than me, but he knew more tricks.

I rolled across the flagstone to clear my head, but he was after me quick as a hot-footed grizzly bear.

As he reached down I jammed my elbow

in his left eye and butted him in the belly.

That slowed him down enough that I could get to my feet and try to see through my one good eye.

He came at me again, powerful and dangerous. With my left eye closed I couldn't get the distance straight in my head, but I threw a right at his solar plexus that I thought couldn't miss.

My hand landed on a slab of muscle and bounced off.

He grunted and stepped forward, starting his haymaker from down at his ankles.

I feinted to the left, then moved inside as the right whistled by my ear, throwing him off balance.

I let loose the left hook I'd been saving and felt my knuckles notch back from the anvil of a jaw.

Still, it made him blink and take a step back, so I tried a right hook that made him shake his head and totter sidewise.

I hit him again twice with the right, but he wouldn't go down. Instead he lurched forward, grabbed me around the waist, pulled me down to the flagstones, and hooked his hands together in a low bear hug that was meant to break my spine.

I jerked and kicked. I arched my back and butted him in the face, but he only increased the pressure with his fists gripped together in the small of my back.

I drove my index finger into his eye, and he winced. I jabbed him in the other eye and butted him again. I felt the pressure lessen and smacked him on the ear with my elbow, then poked his eye again with my thumb, digging it in, trying to get under the eyeball.

He screamed and let loose, staggering to his feet, clawing at his face.

I tottered to my feet, swung a short right with all the shoulder leverage I could muster, and smacked his Adam's apple.

He stumbled, and his mouth gaped open, sucking air. I hit him another one right on the point of the jaw, and he fell back on the flagstones, banging his head hard.

Staggering, I came up with my back against a tree trunk and slid down to sit on my butt, my vision a blur, my lungs burning for air.

It was then that a tall, dark form darted from the shadows. I braced myself stupidly. I couldn't get up.

Lupe ran past me to the groggy Griff Bletcher and showed him the long bowie in her hand. I tried to yell out *No!* but wondered why. I'd wanted to kill him a minute before. Why should I change my mind now?

She made a pass with the knife, and his pants parted neatly in the front. Without hesitation she gripped his genitals in her left hand, pulled taut, and in a hard swipe cut them free.

Standing there a second, she lifted the bloody parts above her head, knife in her right hand poised to stab when I finally hawked up *"No!"*

She stopped, held, turned, and tossed the bloody knife to me, handle first.

I climbed to my feet as she flung the bloody, hairy genitals down the alley where the dogs would find them.

Griff Bletcher was trying to sit up now, one eye open. "What . . ." he groaned weakly.

I lifted him up by the shoulder. "You know where Doc Daud sleeps?"

"Yeah."

"You go on up there, wake him up." I pointed him up the alley toward New Town.

"Why — what . . ." he asked, his head still jumbled.

"Ask him if he can fix you up. Tell him you need help."

"What happened?" he mumbled, pawing a right hand at me.

"Go on!" I gave him a push up the alley.

He took a couple steps. "Doc Daud?"

"Yeah, Doc Daud. Hurry it up before you bleed to death."

I heard him stumbling on up the dark alley. I found my gun and went back to Lupe in the doorway.

"Much woman," I said.

"That *puto cabron* will squat to pee the rest of his miserable life," she muttered, her eyes still burning with fury.

# 11

I went to sleep listening to the mournful howling of dogs discussing the new theory of evolution with distant coyotes, and I awakened listening to the a capella choir of early-rising roosters who sang of their disdain for one another, their own individual artistic talents, and their own pugnacious prowess.

Lying on the roof with dawn swelling up over the east like a golden halo, I tried to sort out the various roosters around the village and valley and noticed how the citified ones politely took turns at standing on their toes, stretching their necks, and screeching their challenge to all roosterdom. But the country cocks pretended there were no village fowl or, simply unhearing, claimed everything under the rising sun.

I smelled freshly roasted coffee, heavy and sweet as chocolate, and climbed out of my lonely bed. I slipped on my boots, gun belt, and hat and went down the ladder to the courtyard, where I could scrub some life into my face and limber up stiffened joints that I'd never noticed before.

The commander had said it was a paid vacation kind of assignment. Nothing to it. Check out a rabble-rouser and let the Rangers handle the hard part. No more screaming dreams, no more kids daring death, no more killings . . . Now it looked like the Rangers were at least half the problem, a fact no one would believe back in Austin. I found myself thinking the best solution for Sam Benbow was to just keep on travelin' west and let the different sides in this war have it out.

Someday you could come back on a steam train and buy a fake arrowhead or a tin badge for a souvenir.

You might ask if there was any memory of a great strong *Mexicana* castrating a massive hog of a man. You'd be met by amused stares. You might ask about a battle for the Contreras rancho, and someone might say, "You mean the Contreras Depot?" You might inquire if anyone had ever heard of a certain lawyer named Marcus Webb who was killed along with a couple *camposinos* for fighting the money-political combine, and someone would no doubt say, "Get that troublemaker out of here."

Thinking along those lines, I found the door to the café open and followed the aroma of freshly made coffee into the kitchen, where Lupe stood over the small fire in a black and white striped robe of some fine homespun material, a black rebozo around her broad, proud shoulders.

The lumps on her face had smoothed down, but the purple bruises tinged with yellow remained.

She looked at me through a crow's wing of glossy hair, murmured, "Good morning, Sam," and poured a cup of coffee for me.

"How are you?" I asked quietly.

"Washed out." She spoke softly. "Maybe I should apologize for my excesses yesterday."

"Why? They brought the battle to you."

"And you and Fortunato and Santos . . ." she murmured. "But I acted more like an animal than a civilized lady."

"You solved some of the problem. Same as we're all trying to do."

"It used to be so peaceful here," she said distantly. "The biggest surprise would be a caravan of ox carts passing through. Everyone would line up along the road and watch them pass by. No one was ever hurt or killed."

"Would you like that backwater peace

back, or would you rather have a railroad build a station here with freight yards and cattle shipping pens?"

"Can't they put it someplace else and leave the valley alone?"

"I'd say it depends on how much you fight."

"I don't know." She shook her head. "I looked in on Santos and the *curandora.* He's better, but he still can hardly speak."

"Nothing?" I asked, surprised.

"Just a few words. I asked him if he had any idea of what the trouble was all about, and he said the man wanted the village archives."

"Yes, sure," I said strongly, "but where are they? And who is this man?"

"He didn't know much. He said he knew the archives were never opened except on November first, but he didn't know why."

"I've got to talk to him. Can you help?"

"I don't think he knows much more." She shrugged. "We can try."

Gathering the hem of her robe up in her hand, she led me out the back way and through the maze of common trails that I was beginning to learn, to the blocky adobe building hidden in the lime trees.

The old lady was back in the kitchen starting a fire, and we looked into Santos's bed-room.

He was sitting up in bed, his hands clasped on his lap. He saw us and lifted a hand to wave us in.

His eyes were partly open, his face recognizable, but he wasn't saying anything.

I didn't waste much time on good morning pleasantries. "Ask him if he has any idea who did this to him."

She spoke in soft, liquid Spanish, and Santos replied in a whisper.

Lupe turned. "He says no, he never got to see him."

"Ask him if there is something he can remember — anything — about the man."

Again she spoke rapidly, but in phrases close and familiar to him. He put his head back against a pillow and stared at the opposite wall for half a minute, then, without moving, croaked out, "The man spoke in a false voice in Spanish."

"Nothing else?" I asked. "Tell him to take his time."

Again Santos studied the opposite wall, then, in that painful, rasping voice he spoke again to Lupe.

"He says the man walked back and forth. He heard boots instead of huaraches. He said the man kicked him with his boot, so the man couldn't be one of us."

"Did he give the man a name? A place to go?" I tried my last wild idea.

Santos lifted his burned hands to his face in an act of shame, and tears ran down his gaunt cheeks. After a while he nodded and croaked out, "Tio Ignacio."

"Who is Tio Ignacio?" I asked.

"He is a very old man who is everyone's uncle. He is known as a *brujo blanco.*"

"A witch doctor?"

"Sort of — only the *blanco* is the good kind. He never does harm. He only makes good luck for all things — money, love, health — whatever you want."

"Would he know where the archives are kept?"

Santos understood me and needed no translation. He nodded yes, then added, "The Day of the Dead."

"We'd better look in on Tio Ignacio and see if he's in any better shape than Santos."

Lupe patted Santos on the shoulder and he croaked, *"Apurate —"*

"He said hurry up," she muttered, leading me on a winding path that took us into a yard covered by a ramada from which hung a multitude of wooden bird cages filled with varicolored finches and odd sparrows, as well as a couple of warblers and orioles.

230

The house might have been the oldest building in town. The mortar between the adobe bricks had eroded away, leaving geometric seams crisscrossing the walls.

Lupe knocked at a thin, paneled door that could have been painted red a hundred years ago.

There was no answer, and she pushed the door open.

In the first light of morning we saw the old man sitting in a hard kitchen chair. His white-bearded face was slumped down over his chest. The only thing holding him up was the length of rawhide reata binding him to the chair.

He was cold to the touch, his body stiff in rigor mortis.

"Oh, *Madre de Dios,*" Lupe moaned, tears in her eyes. "He was such a good man."

The room was clean and simple. There were packages of herbs, feathers, and bones and a stuffed hummingbird on a shelf. The place wasn't torn up by a search, but the bony hands showed the same cigar burns that blistered Santos's hands.

The killer had wasted no time. Once he'd gotten the name from Santos he'd come over here, tied up the old man, and lighted up another stogie. He hadn't blindfolded the old *brujo blanco* because once he'd gotten his information he meant to kill him.

From the number of burns on the hands and thin arms it looked like the old man had held back for a long time.

"You think he told where the archives are?" Lupe asked.

I didn't want to point out the loop of rawhide reata buried in the old man's neck that had been cinched up tight.

"It's a good guess." I nodded. "Or he'd still be burning polka dots on the old man."

"I've got to tell the village elders," she said.

I waited for her outside another adobe house while she went in to report to Don Jaime Reyes.

When she returned she said, "He'll take care of it. He is calling a meeting."

"In the schoolhouse?" I asked.

"No. He wants to have it at the church."

We went through the courtyard and into the café's secure shadows, a haven in a paradise that had turned into hell.

I'd been hoping that somewhere along the line she'd say something about us, something about the passion of only forty-eight hours before, but she said nothing. It seemed blanked from her mind.

With her hair uncombed, wearing the old robe, she looked more like a middle-aged housewife worried about the price of beans than the powerful, vibrant, handsome woman I had known before.

I'd never pretended to understand the female state of mind or condition, having been led over too many rocky roads by the irrational whims of ladies with usually good common sense, but this transformation stretched my experience. I thought if I could just manage my own manhood, I'd be lucky.

After a quiet breakfast of *huevos rancheros* she went off into her room and left me to contemplate the unpredictable female or the follies of my life, both equally unrewarding and depressing. Better to find Skofer and clear out while we were still alive, I thought.

What stake had we in this little valley? They'd run it without us for hundreds of years. Why change? I'd had a notion that Lupe and I could make some kind of a life there, but I couldn't see myself in white cotton and huaraches irrigating a melon patch.

Heavy thinking made me jumpy and sore as a bobtailed bull in fly time.

Darn women anyway, I had my own aches and pains, too, a lot more than when I had ridden into this town.

I left by the front door, daring anybody to try to put me under arrest. There were no Rangers on the street, only a couple of ladies sweeping up leaves and throwing out buckets of water to keep down the dust.

I walked up to the edge of New Town to Mrs. Kapp's Windsor House and went up the steps to the veranda, where Skofer sat in a rocking chair, a soft blanket over his knees, a cup of tea on the table at his elbow.

"Mornin', Sam," he said in a weak, apologetic tone.

"Don't give me none of that sad Skofer sauce," I said gruffly. "You had your choice, and you picked the rockin' chair instead of a man's way."

"I been crippled up, Sam," he said plaintively.

"Sounds like you think you can change your mind like a danged female," I replied sharply. "No, if I was to take on a sidekick, I'd have to have one I could count on when the bullets started flying."

"Sam —" he squeaked.

"You've got everything your lazy hide ever wanted right here. I'm pleased for you. Not many no-account old coots come out on top like you have."

He looked over his shoulder and whispered, "She reads the Bible in bed."

"I expect you find that highly edifying," I said, "and I just bet you sleep like a long-bearded prophet next to the promised land."

"I'm fit to travel," he protested.

"Skofer?" Mrs. Kapp called from the vestibule. "What do you want now?"

"No, little lambkin," he called back, "it's just an old friend come to pay his last respects."

"Who?" She barged out the door. "Oh — you." She frowned like a bulldog with a bellyache.

"Yes'm."

"You tryin' to toll him away?" She glared at me.

"No, ma'am, I don't have no need of such a frail, gutless critter."

Skofer flinched and hung his head.

"You take him," she said emphatically. "He's no good around here."

"What's the trouble, ma'am?"

"No spunk. No grit. Likes to lay around and languish during workin' hours. Tell him to wash out the chamber pots — he develops the colic. Tell him to boil water — he don't know how and don't want to learn —"

"I should have warned you," I said. "I can't do nothin' about it now."

"You'd best take him off my hands," she barked, setting her hands on her large hams, leaning toward me, "or I'll put a bee up your butt so fast, you'll be wondering which way the wind is blowin'!"

"That sounds some indelicate, ma'am, but

I'm awful busy this week — can't you keep him a little longer?"

"If you don't take him, I'm going to have to throw him down the stairs," she declared, her face mottled with red spots, "and I ain't going down to pick up the pieces neither."

"Looks like you're *persona au gratin,* Skofey," I said.

"Anything you say, Sam." He nodded mournfully, laid the blanket aside, and slowly rose to his feet, making a big show of his creaking knees and bowed-over back.

"If he can't set a horse, I can't use him," I said, starting down the stairs.

In a second he was bounding down the steps, and he passed me halfway down.

"Amazing what fresh air will do for a body," he cackled, prancing around like a fat pony in tall oats.

"You old fool!" she squalled after him. "You couldn't even pour pee out of a boot!"

"Lady's some disappointed in you, Skofey. Maybe you better go back and give lambkin a little kiss."

"I'd sooner kiss the hind end of a mean mule!" He grinned, showing his worn-off teeth.

"Knee all healed up?"

"Mister, I stood up before I was weaned, I got hair all over my brisket, and I'm all

236

heart above and all guts below!" he yipped, flexing his muscles like he was some kind of fightin' fool.

"Maybe you can help hold off them Rangers whilst I look around town."

"You know me, pard, you can count on old Skofe. I know how to die standin' up!"

"Keep your eyes open for that Sergeant Krimpke. He's probably worryin' about me walkin' around the streets in broad daylight."

"I heard about that big shitepoke Bletcher," Skofer said.

"I didn't do it."

"But you had words?"

"You could say that." I nodded as we walked down the main street of Old Town toward the boxy church, where a crowd was gathering.

Coming closer, I saw that Father Salinski, dressed in a black suit and reversed collar, was surrounded by the villagers.

"The man wore boots, Santos says." An old bearded man was speaking slowly.

"Of course I wear boots," Salinski said angrily, "but I wouldn't torture anyone!"

"You been tellin' us to turn in the archives," another man said, shoving up close to the priest.

"I think it's best for the village, Domingo,"

Salinski said nervously.

"You smoke cigars!" another ferocious-looking man growled.

"Lots of people smoke cigars!"

"You hated Tio Ignacio!"

"True, I disliked his witchcraft, but I wouldn't kill him!"

"You would if you could get the papers, too," old Jaime Reyes said firmly. "Where are they?"

"I don't have them."

"You better start tellin' the truth, or we're goin' to make a saint out of you," another burly man with one eye growled.

The women, dressed in black and coiffed with their *rebozos,* stood aside, watching and waiting like a silent jury. I noted Lupe stood abjectly in the back of the group, her eyes downcast.

Salinski yelled, backing up, "Now don't you start something you can't finish!"

"You damned murderer!" Domingo yelled, and shoved him back against the wall.

*"Joto!"* Another jammed his fist against the cleric's chest.

"Now wait! All I've ever done was to try to better this community. To bring goodness and progress into your hearts side by side!"

238

"And hand over our property to the banker," Jaime Reyes said sharply.

"I'm leaving!" Salinski cried out, suddenly giving way under the anger of the crowd. "You cannot punish a man of the cloth, or you'll all go straight to hell!"

"Kill the *joto!*" one of the women cried out, and the crowd surged forward.

"No! No! Please, I'll go! I want to go, I hate this stinking little stupid, worthless peasant hole!"

Salinski backed through the door and slammed it shut, yelling, "Keep your mud brick church! Keep your witch doctor! Keep your crazy holidays! Keep your sinful ways! You can all go to hell for all I care! You'll never see me again!"

The crowd stood silently, then commenced fading away.

"I guess that finishes Salinski," I said.

"He'll be lucky to get out with his skin intact." Skofer nodded. "Wrong man in the wrong place at the wrong time."

"Likely," I nodded. "You know Spanish, Skofer — what would you reckon *el punto* means so far as a hiding place?"

"Point. Period. The end of your tally-whacker. It means one out of twelve things in a line, too, but that won't help. I'd judge it'd have to be a point."

"Like a peak?"

"Could be. The top of a peak." He nodded.

"There aren't any peaks around here," I said, shaking my head.

"There's the hill there," he said, nodding up at the graveyard.

I thought about it. The colorful grave markers and miniature chapels where Marcus Webb was buried.

I crossed over to Lupe, who was starting to leave, and asked, "What was Tio Ignacio's last name?"

"Villavicencio. He was the last of the family."

"Thanks." I nodded and took Skofer by the arm, leading him toward the cemetery.

"You know who killed him?" he asked when we were free of the group.

"Maybe, but I'll bet I know for sure where that box of documents is kept."

We hurried up the trail that wound around the low hill and passed through the narrow gate into the graveyard itself. Nothing much had changed. The three graves had been filled in and temporary headboards set up.

I went on past to the central part, which was a little higher than the rest, and saw the miniature pink, white, and blue chapel built over a grave. It was old, but it had been repainted every year on All Souls Day so that it looked fairly new.

Over the small door, chiseled in stone, was the name:

## VILLAVICENCIO

One day a year the people cleaned the graves, dusted out the locked chapels, and painted them. On that day Tio Ignacio had looked in each year to see that the box of documents stored in his chapel was secure and unharmed. That day was All Souls Day, November first.

"That's it, the top of the top," I said.

Skofer noticed the broken lock, an ancient, over-sized brass piece, first.

"Tad late," he murmured.

I swung open the door and peered inside. Anchored to a flat rock slab a corroded hammered copper box lay with its lid pried off. It was empty.

There was nothing else inside except an ancient dried wreath made of rosemary branches.

I stepped back and closed the door.

"Gone!" I shook my head. "I can guess where —"

"Where?" came the gravelly voice of big Sergeant Krimpke.

I turned slowly to face him.

"You alone?" I asked, surprised.

"I don't share the pot," he said, a slow smile growing on his broad, beefy face.

"You thought I'd lead you to the archives, and you'd just take 'em and sell 'em?"

"You could make an honest livin' readin' minds," he said. "Now where are they?"

"You can follow along," I said. "I'll take you right there."

"I said I don't share. You just tell me and then get out of town while you're still in one piece."

"Tell him," Skofer said. "It's not our fight."

"Listen to the wise old bird." Krimpke took a step closer.

"I'm not goin' to fight you," I said. "I think you're better than Bletcher, and I'm feelin' a little puny today."

"You cut Bletch?" Krimpke asked, taking another step forward.

"Not me, but I ruined my left hand on his bone head, and my right isn't much better."

"There's no way out of it, though — is there?" He grinned, reaching out for my shirtfront.

"You're wearin' a gun," I said quickly, moving back again.

Skofer was unarmed and moved to one

side, likely thinking he'd jump on top of the big bastard and bite his neck.

"I don't like the odds," Krimpke said. "I'd rather just stomp your guts out."

"I'll kill you first, Krimpke." I backed another step, my right hand poised to draw.

"I guess you'd like to try." He laughed this time, and I stepped back again as Skofer yelled a warning.

Too late I felt the low headstone touch the back of my knees.

As I went backwards I tried to draw, but Krimpke launched a flying leap at me that pinned me to the ground with his extra weight.

Sure enough, Skofer made a dive at his back and grabbed his right arm as he started a sledgehammer fist at my head.

Like a big bear with a terrier Krimpke threw Skofer through the sky, and I heard a thunk as Skofer landed against a stone crypt.

Krimpke was astride me, his knees pinning my wrists down. My right hand had the six-gun butt, but I couldn't bring it up to fire.

He started the right hand again, and I took the only chance I had.

Pulling the trigger of the holstered Colt, I sent off a wild bullet that might just have gone into my leg or, with the help of Providence, might nick the foot of the big bull of a man astride me.

He jerked sideways, a surprised look on his face.

Glancing over his shoulder, he eased off his knee pressure just enough that I could bend the holster to the side and pull the trigger again.

This one smacked him just below the knee and hurt him.

He swung the right fist, but he was off balance, and I jerked my head sideways, taking the graze on the side of the head. I hitched my hand another fraction to the left and fired again.

This slug broke his thigh bone just above the knee, and he rolled aside, clawing for his own six-gun.

He drew with overanxious desperation, firing before he was set. The bullet screamed by my ear, and powder grains burned the side of my face, but I had time to fire with his whole bulk as my target.

The slug took him right under the sternum and blew his upper stomach back through his backbone. The shock of the muzzle blast slammed him over backwards, and Skofe made a dive to wrench the gun free from the massive right hand.

I got to my knees and looked into the blocky, broken features squeezing hard against the pain.

He let out a long, discordant belch and groaned as the right hand drifted over to the wound and gripped hard.

I climbed to my feet and leaned against a crypt, trying to get my breath as he twisted his head from one side to the other.

He tried to roll onto his side, but the broken leg wouldn't work. He glared up at me, his yellow teeth bared, and screamed, "You!"

"It's too late, sergeant," I murmured.

"Why?!" He yelled so loud it echoed back from the ridge to the west. Then he arched his back like a bow and commenced kicking wildly, his boots flailing the tall wild oats.

# 12

I reloaded as we hurried off that sorry, gaudy hill.

Skofer, dragging behind, croaked, "Slow yourself down, old hoss."

I stopped and waited for him to catch up. He was right. I'd been going like a runaway wild horse, and whenever a horse chucks away what little sense he has and goes into motion you can bet he'll get himself hurt.

"Goin' crazy," I said. "It's the killin' fever. I got to break it."

"Sure enough — but that box of papers won't blow away. You know where you're going?"

"The schoolhouse." I picked up the pace again. "It should be over there in the trees."

As we turned into the lane that led to the school we met a group of boys and girls coming from the other way.

"*¿Donde está la escuela, por favor?*" Skofer asked a round-eyed boy wearing the traditional white pants and shirt.

*"Allá."* He pointed back. *"Pero, el Maestro no está."*

*"Porque?"* Skofer asked.

*"No se."* The boy shrugged his small shoulders so eloquently it seemed to me they must teach shoulder shrugging along with reading and writing.

Skofer passed on the boy's shrug, then hustled to keep up with me.

We passed through a *huerta* of apple and pear trees and found the building, which was divided into a schoolroom and rooms for the teacher's residence.

I took a quick look into the schoolroom, where there were the usual tables and benches, and a map of Mexico before 1836 hanging alongside a black slate upon which was lettered *Hoy no escuela.*

I opened the door leading to Tiburcio Bernal's room. Clutter of books, unwashed dishes, clothes, boots, abacuses, and slates, but empty of Tiburcio Bernal.

"He's already makin' a deal," I said.

"How can you be so sure he's the one?" Skofer asked doubtfully.

"The boots. Santos heard them on the board floor when he was blindfolded."

"Could have been a *gringo* or the priest —"

"No, he said his Spanish was local, only he changed his voice. There's only one local in this valley that doesn't wear huaraches, and that's our schoolmaster."

"Why would he sell out the town?" Skofer followed me out into the lane again.

"He likes shiny boots and everything that goes along with them. He learned it when he went to college in St. Louis, and he's been feeling superior ever since he got back. The problem was, no one paid him any attention, including Lupe."

"But why would he try to provoke a massacre up in the graveyard?"

"He hates these people, believe me. He would have dived into one of the graves if it had come to a slaughter, and he'd have come out smelling like a rose."

I cut across a harvested bean field, going as straight as possible for the tall buildings of New Town.

"They'll have heard the shooting," Skofer cautioned me. "It won't do to just bull down the middle of Main Street."

"I am going to get that damn box of papers!" I said loud and clear.

"Sam, I'm not carrying a weapon," Skofer murmured as we came out at the foot of Main Street.

I stopped to get my head clear. There was

Mrs. Kapp's Windsor House, then the Lone Star Saloon. Across the street was the First National Bank of Texas, and on the corner the big mercantile.

At the end of the street was the livery stable, with a corral next to it and a stack of hay on beyond.

There was no one on the street.

What bothered me were the men lounging in doorways in such a way that I couldn't see who they were or what they were doing.

"What do you make of it?" I asked Skofe.

"I'd say the Rangers are expectin' some damn galoot to come charging up Main Street with his six-gun blazin'," Skofer said, studying the street, which should have been busy with riders and wagons, ladies shopping, kids playing.

"Skofe," I said, "I've got to get over to that bank building before it's all over."

"What you got in mind besides suicide?"

I told him and said I'd give him two minutes to get it done.

After he'd gone I tried counting the shadows of men I couldn't see. It looked like six, but it might have been ten or twelve.

I thought if they put a couple sharpshooters up on the hotel's second floor, I might as well turn around and go home, but I had a certain notion Mrs. Kapp would object to a bunch of gunmen messin' up her rooms.

Only way was to give it a try.

I saw the smoke first because I was looking for it.

A second later I heard someone yell, "Fire! Fire in the livery!"

That brought the shadows out into the street and turned them into gunmen carrying carbines.

From their point of view the hay burning on beyond looked like it was coming from the barn itself, where the horses were stalled.

I counted eight Rangers running up the middle of the street toward the barn.

I followed along after them, moving down the boardwalk, keeping close to the buildings, trying to look like I was minding my own business.

When I was opposite the bank building I ambled on across with my shoulder blades wide open and inviting to any sharpshooter that had been left behind.

Halfway across I thought it was too easy. Something had to go wrong.

Still in one piece, I arrived on the corner and then had to decide whether Tiburcio Bernal was in the bank with Sharp or upstairs with ex–Senator Alfred Slade.

I guessed wrong. I went up the three stone

steps and meant to take a quick look in the bank, then try the stairway to the office upstairs, but as I stood with one hand holding the door open Captain Ogden Zanger faced me with his army Colt at the ready. Alongside him stood Corporal Sidney, his scar-padded, poker-playing eyes set on my gun hand.

Far back I saw the banker, B. G. Sharp, standing, his fingers drumming nervously on his potbelly, a sweet smile on his pink face.

"You're under arrest," Zanger said crisply. "Hand over your gun very carefully."

"Any particular charge?" I asked, not moving, my weight still balanced on my left foot, my hand on the door handle.

"Call it three counts of murder." He smiled, contempt all over his face.

"Where's Bernal?" I asked.

"Upstairs. It's all over," Zanger sneered. "I offered you a chance to make a fortune, but you preferred to play the fool —"

I spun left on my boot toe, slammed the door closed, and ducked low just as the two six-guns fired, punching splinters through the oak panel.

I drew and spaced three slugs waist-high across the door, figuring I could play that game, too.

My second shot brought a grunt like that of a pig kicked in the butt from one of them. My third brought a sharp cry of pain from Corporal Sidney.

Now was the moment to make or break, the crucial second where you play wild to win or you play cool to stay even. Staying even meant losing to me, and feeling the cutting edge of mortal combat scraping at my network of instincts, I grabbed open the door again with my free hand and flung myself aside.

In that brief glimpse I saw Zanger on the floor, his right hand clutching at his lower right side, trying to stem the flow of his body fluids.

On one knee Sidney was looking in awe at his left hand, where my bullet had clipped off his little finger.

It took him a second to get his mind back onto business and fire through the open door. It was too long. I snapped a shot low and another high, then stepped back to reload.

Sidney pitched halfway out the door, a neat hole marking his scarred left cheekbone, his cold eyes now as flat and homeless as blue poker chips.

I took a quick look inside and saw Zanger beckoning. I moved in slowly, half expecting a third gunman hiding out, but there was only Sharp standing where he'd been, his hands now clutching at the vest pockets like he wanted to hold himself up straight.

I knelt over Zanger and looked into his faded eyes. Blood and paunch juice spurted through his fingers.

"Benbow," he coughed, "what went wrong?"

"You, captain."

"But, who —"

"It's a little late."

It wasn't worth telling a dying man that he couldn't grade humans like cattle into culls, cutters, and canners, and then prime, and then divine. He'd thought the Bernardeños were lazy, stupid farmers, beneath respect or equal rights. He saw himself as superior, intelligent, decisive, well-off, secure, all adding up to elite. Once the top dogs start thinking they're in the elite, they right away start thinking they're the next thing to being the second coming of the Son of God, and whatever they do is right. Not only right, but necessary to keep the elite elite, the divine divine.

"Yes, a little late . . . someone will look after my family?"

"I'm sure."

"Watch him!" Skofer yelled from the

253

doorway, and I looked up to see banker Sharp's right hand coming clear of his coat, a two-shot derringer palmed in his hand.

I rolled forward as he fired. The heavy slug caught my left forearm, then passed into the top of Zanger's head, shutting off his elite divinity, as it would for anyone else.

Sharp saw he'd missed and ran sideways for the safety of the counter, but his short legs couldn't reach out fast enough, and my second slug took him through the hips.

The derringer went flying off to the corner as he slid across the floor.

I stood, looking at my bleeding left arm. It was a flesh wound that stung like hell. Skofer made two quick turns around the wound with his bandanna and tied it tight.

"Let's get on out of here, Sam," he said anxiously.

"We're not done yet." I looked around at the room, making sure none of this cat meat would resurrect and shoot me in the back.

Reloading again, I stepped out onto the boardwalk and saw that the street was still quiet. None of the pissant newcomers were willing to haul out a rifle and start blazing away just yet. They wanted to be sure they were on the winning side first.

I stepped around to the wooden stairway that went up to Slade's office and then caught myself and jerked back.

A slug speared the space where I'd just been and went howling as it ricocheted on across the street.

There was no time left for battle strategies or tactics. No time for conscience searching, no time for questioning that ancient dictum "Thou shalt not kill." No time to say the bodies are too many, the blood too deep.

The remnants of the Ranger force would be coming back down the street in a few seconds, and any one of them was expert with carbine and revolver.

I threw myself across the space without thinking or saying one two three, so that I landed somersaulting in the cross street. The second bullet went where the first had gone, and I saw a figure on the landing aiming a long blue barrel down at me as I snapped my quickest shot, doing whatever desperate thing I could do to distract his aim.

His bullet tore a chunk of muscle out of my right thigh, but I'd come close enough so that he ran back into the office.

Grabbing the handrail, I hobbled up the stairway one step at a time, probably sounding like the bass drum of doom coming ever closer.

I saw a shadow off to my left and started to whirl and fire when I heard Skofer's "No!" blasting through my red ferocity.

It was Lupe coming at a run, her dress held above her knees, screaming at me. "Wait! Come back, Sam!"

I couldn't wait, I couldn't lose my rage. It was the wrong time for a lecture on love and honor.

With unreckoning fire, I win. The spider's way, the plan, the web, the wait, the bite, I lose. If I must go, I will go in fire.

Leaving a track of my liquid life behind on every step, I hauled myself up the stairs, my eyes set on the landing and the door beyond, my Colt up and ready.

Damn it! I thought, why does it have to be so hard? Why couldn't they be down on the level where the old man didn't have to stop and catch his breath every four or five steps? He'd be a wide-open target when he came to the landing itself.

Whoever dealt this hand was giving me low cards in odd colors.

"Come out!" I yelled for the hell of it.

You never know . . . some jaspers, big and full of beans, will fall apart when they know a man with a gun is coming after them. All bluff and bravado, they're really hoping someone will call out, "Come out with your hands up!" because they know they'll have a chance to talk themselves clear.

Slade and Bernal could well be that type of hombre. Not that I was absolutely certain Slade and Bernal were up there in the office, but I couldn't think of any better place.

Pico Bernal wore glossy boots and the finery of St. Louis gents. He was a cheroot smoker, an educated man, a reader of Cervantes, Montaigne, and Machiavelli. This was the man who'd been forced to return to San Bernardo and teach farm kids. He couldn't stand to hear Bernardo, talk Bernardo, drink Bernardo, eat Bernardo, and most of all couldn't bear the thought he'd die Bernardo.

Even Lupe, the Thoroughbred amongst mustangs, would not acknowledge his distinguished career nor yield him the subservient love he thought he deserved.

He was smart enough to see that he didn't belong in San Bernardo, but he needed money to move. It wouldn't be hard to figure that the squat little ignorant village owed him and, by rights, should pay his way out.

He'd figured the old dumbheads who took him for granted and teased him for his long nose were standing in his way with their secrets, blocking him from achieving the honors he deserved.

Sure of his rightness, he'd stalked Alfonso and Santos and finally the old *brujo blanco,* Tio Ignacio, and convinced them, in his own way, that he was right.

I heard Lupe yelling behind me at the bottom of the stairs, and Skofer yelling right back, "No, dang it, woman!"

The last thing I needed was for a highly charged, emotional woman to get in the way. Skofer was keeping her out of it. Of course, he wouldn't last long, I thought. She'd beat him to doll rags in a minute or two.

It seemed to me I was slowing down, getting lightheaded, and I kicked my lazy mental butt and told it to get movin'.

A shot blew splinters off the handrail next to my left hand. Instinctively I jerked back and looked for a hidden rifle.

Another shot screamed in over my head. I dropped down, hoping the balustrade would screen me from the riflemen.

It had to be the returning Rangers. They had me pinned halfway up the stairs with their long-range weapons.

All of a sudden it was a turkey shoot, and I was the bird.

Two more quick ones broke through the spindles above me. They were guessing.

There were three of them holed up on the other side of the mercantile, out of my six-gun range.

A couple more had Skofer and Lupe pinned down where the landing turned at the boardwalk.

I tried to crawl up a step, but my right leg spoke up against it.

You can't do that to me, it said.

The hell I can't, you son of a bitch, I thought. I made it go up the step just to prove who was boss. The pain came back at me with nausea in my belly and sudden cold sweat breaking out over my whole body.

Now they were picking away at the bottom and moving their sights up the banister, meaning to flush me off the stairway one way or another.

I almost forgot to keep my mind on the landing above me.

I saw the shiny gray sleeve, the gleam of metal, the belch of flame and smoke. I fired close and low, trying to hit some part of the body. Any kind of wound would help me out. Neither of those two up there were gunmen, and the sight of their own blood might break their nerve.

There was no cry or whimper of pain from the doorway above, but at least the gunman had reconsidered his position.

With the riflemen blowing the balustrade to splinters, I couldn't afford to wait until their unrolling carpet of fire tore me to pieces.

The slats just below me exploded as the .44-40s bloomed and blew their way that much closer.

Gritting my teeth, I hoisted myself another step, hugging the wall of the building, trying to squeeze out another ounce of strength, another foot of elevation.

The next fusillade never came. Instead I heard more distant firing and men yelling.

Taking a quick look through the balustrade, I saw riders on Spanish mules and mustangs entering the street. The riders, dressed in white, wearing dumpy straw hats, carried machetes and carbines, and slung across their breasts were crisscrossed bandoliers of ammunition.

Their carbines bloomed. Machetes gleamed and glittered. Rangers were legging it down the street, aiming for the alley behind the Lone Star Saloon.

I glimpsed the round porkpie face of Kiko leading the riders, a ferocious scowl on his otherwise placid features.

That was good enough for me. Grabbing the banister, I hauled myself up and got my feet under me. This way the leg might go under protest, but it would go.

I was four steps from the top when the .44 at the end of the gray, shiny sleeve poked out again. He didn't aim; he just pointed blindly where he thought I'd be and pulled the trigger.

He guessed wrong. My own bullet splattered against the six-gun's grips and then tore off half the pink hand.

I heard Slade's bellow of pain and came up another step, figuring he still had another hand.

I reached the landing, took a breath, leaned far over, and turned the doorknob.

"Come in! Don't shoot!" I heard Slade yell. "I'm bleeding to death!"

I swung open the door from the side, giving whoever was waiting no target.

"Kick that gun out here, Slade!"

"Oh, hell! Take the damn gun! Get the doctor!"

"Not yet, mister." I took off my hat and showed it in the door. Nothing.

Coming in as fast as the leg would go, I fired blindly into the room, hoping to mix up whatever scheme was operating against me.

Slade was sitting in the secretary's chair, his hand bleeding through a towel wrapped around it.

His fat, yellow face was pale, his breath coming short and quick from his bloated chest. His thick lips were gray and twitching with fear.

"I need a doctor! Quick!" he moaned.

"Where's Tiburcio Bernal?" I asked, keeping the six-gun aimed at the far open door. I could see Slade's big walnut desk. It was the only hiding place left.

"Gone — ran off when we heard the first shot. He's halfway to Mexico City."

That's where he'd head for, I thought. A satchel full of money would set him up nicely with the high-class crooks in the capital of his choosing.

"Did you give him the ten thousand dollars?"

"Please!" Slade lifted the bleeding towel, exposing flesh, tendons, and white bone fragments. "A doctor!"

"Did you?"

"Yes! It had to be that way! Old Contreras somehow got reinforced, and that cattleman Durham disappeared."

"It doesn't make any difference then which way the rail line goes, just so long as it goes?"

"Right!"

"You'd spoil this little valley just to make the railroad planners content."

"You break eggs to make an omelette," he groaned.

"Where are the archives?"

"Gone!" Sweat was beading his bulging gray forehead, his squat form pressed against the desk.

"You don't want a doctor," I said, starting to turn away.

"All right! They're here," he bellowed, and he pulled an old walnut box out from under the desk. It had heavy brass hardware; on the lid was the elegantly carved seal of royal Spain.

I thought I knew how it would go, but you can never really set yourself exactly. There are too many variations on main moves.

He balanced the box in his left hand, then threw it square in my face. Even though I was ready I didn't react quickly enough to the left-handed pitch.

Bernal came up from behind the far desk with a short two-bore twelve-gauge blazing.

A buckshot cut my right ear as I dropped. The other nineteen macerated the back of the thick neck and domed head of Alfred Slade, attorney at law, former senator, former railroad front man.

"I quit! Don't shoot!" Bernal yelled, throwing the empty shotgun out on the floor.

I slid around on my belly and covered him.

Bernal stood behind Slade's broad desk, his long arms hanging down so I couldn't see his hands. "Get your hands high!" I snapped.

Standing straight in his best checkered suit and high-heeled boots, he looked down his long nose at me and said contemptuously, "I surrender. Why should I put my hands up?"

"Up!" I yelled, danger screaming in my ears. "Up, you bastard! I'll shoot!"

*"Tu pinche. . . ."*

I gave him one more chance, more than I'd give most. "Up, goddamnit! Up or you're dead!"

He stared at me with all the hatred in his hateful heart.

I shot him right there. The red stain spread over the left breast of his cheap suit. He fell forward across the glossy walnut desk.

I waited for the thunk of a hidden gun falling. It didn't come.

I picked up the carved box, tucked it under my left arm, and holstered my six-gun. I thought I'd surely killed enough for that day, enough for a couple of lifetimes, enough to set my hands to trembling, my shoulders to shaking.

Lupe came legging into the office and grabbed me in a great hug, and I winced.

"Oh! You poor, sweet man!" she cried out incoherently. She was a very high-strung woman even for a Bernardeña.

Skofe showed up, then Kiko, his mustache angling fiercely down on either side of his grim mouth.

I gave him the box. "The deeds and documents should be in there."

He nodded and opened the box to check.

"Thank you, *señor*," he said, smiling.

We moved down the stairway, a weary, happy knot of people. I felt the leaden letdown that always comes after a fight. I just wanted to get my scratches cleaned out, scrub my hands with sand and lye soap, throw my six-gun in the river, then sleep for a week.

We were on the boardwalk across from the Lone Star Saloon when the batwing doors burst open and young Ogden Zanger, Jr. stepped out.

If he hadn't been so dangerous, I would have laughed. He wore two black gunbelts crossed, two tied-down holstered Colts on his thighs. His hands were held chest high.

"Benbow!" he yelled, trying to keep his voice low. "Step clear!"

I lifted my hands and nodded at Skofe and

Lupe to move off. I stepped down into the street.

"I don't want to fight you, son," I called back. "My fight with your dad was fair and square."

"Luck!" he yelled back. "Now try me!"

"No. No, I won't."

"I'm faster'n you! I shoot straighter!"

"I'm tellin' you I won't!" I yelled, strong as I could without making him any madder than he was. "I mean it. I'm finished, burned out. Leave me be! You win!"

He lifted the left-hand Colt, limber-armed and quick as a snake, and fired on the rise, the bullet ticking my shirtsleeve. He squeezed off four more rapid-fire like that, just missing my hide here and there.

When it was empty he holstered the Colt and smiled at me wickedly. "Next time I draw, I'm goin' to punch your guts out your yella backstraps!"

I believed him.

He didn't give me any time to answer.

I caught the shoulder twitch and whirled left a half turn, blending my rising hand with the blue steel weapon, bringing it up as his own gun came a shade faster.

Old, I thought, old and slow and unwilling . . . even as I was touching the trigger. But backed into the angle of life and death, the most primitive of inner voices spoke up for life, my life.

His bullet burned across my shoulder blades right where he'd meant to put it, except I'd turned, and my front wasn't the target.

Without knowing or thinking, my Colt roared and bucked and dented his brocade vest.

His next bullet went into the street as he fell.

Life was running out of his eyes when I knelt and looked into his young face, wishing in that moment that I could shoot straight enough to pick each shot.

"Nice shift," he gritted, trying to sound like a good loser.

But this wasn't that kind of game. While he struggled to hold the smile unbidden tears leaked from his eyes. He tried to blink them away, then screamed in a boy's voice, "It hurts like hell!"

He slumped loose and limber in the horse manure and dust of Main Street, and I looked into the unmarked chalky face of a sleeping boy.

# EPILOGUE

I felt a nagging worry that something was going on that I didn't know anything about, and I mentioned it to Skofer as we lounged in Lupe's courtyard.

"You just won't never settle down and enjoy the fun," he said grumpily. "We never had such peace and quiet in such a pretty place with such fine company. Now you're gettin' itchy already!"

"You're right." I nodded. "Tell me again about the railroad and Don Fortunato."

"You tell him, Lupe. I want to sample this watermelon," Skofe grumbled.

"The negotiators for the railroad came and talked to the elders here and to Don Fortunato. They decided if Don Fortunato would sell them a square mile down at the old crossroads, they'd just let us wither away." She smiled.

I noticed a certain serenity and confidence in her manner that was overcoming her usual outgoing show of vigorous strength and figured she was beginning to take me for granted after two weeks of healing up on the roof.

It was more than the knitting of torn muscles, it was the washing away of that young boy's face from my mind.

I told her it was gone, that there was nothing there, and then she'd shake me in the middle of the night and tell me to stop crying.

*Poco a poco.* Little by little. You got to keep chewin' till you can swallow it. Best think about starting a family, raising some youngsters of your own that'll do something worthwhile with their lives. . . .

"What will happen to us?" she murmured.

"You can sell travelers all your produce," I said. "You'll make a little money, but be careful of that stuff. Sometimes it's worse'n poison."

"You know what we do with it?" she teased.

"Tell me."

"We bury it a long time until, like good red wine, it is aged enough to properly enjoy."

"You think we ought to report to the commander about them Texas Rangers?" Skofer asked.

"I don't figure they were the pure quill. I figure Captain Zanger got mixed up with Slade and went bad."

"Marcus Webb didn't believe they had any authority." Skofer nodded.

"We have named the new school Marcus Webb School. Underneath his name is his motto, *Vincit omnia veritas,*" Lupe said, pacing the floor nervously.

I got up from the pigskin chair, walked over to the lime tree, and smelled the heavy perfume of its tiny white blossoms.

Turning around, I took Lupe's hand in mine and looked down at the flagstones.

Skofer took the hint and wandered off through the orchard.

"Don't tell me," Lupe said, turning to face me. "I know you can't settle down here."

"There's nothing much for me to do, even if I call it home," I said, looking her in the eyes and telling her straight.

"I'll bet you can't even stay long enough to make a blue-eyed baby," she said, tossing her hair, making it a challenge.

"What'll you bet?" I smiled.

# ABOUT THE AUTHOR

**Jack Curtis** was born at Lincoln Center, Kansas. At an early age he came to live in Fresno, California. He served in the U.S. Navy during the Second World War, with duty in the Pacific theater. He began writing short stories after the war for the magazine market. Sam Peckinpah, later a film director, had also come from Fresno, and he enlisted Curtis in writing teleplays and story adaptations for *Dick Powell's Zane Grey Theater.* Sometimes Curtis shared credit for these teleplays with Peckinpah; sometimes he did not. Other work in the television industry followed with Curtis writing episodes for *The Rifleman, Have Gun, Will Travel,* Sam Peckinpah's *The Westerner, Rawhide, The Outlaws, Wagon Train, The Big Valley, The Virginian* and *Gunsmoke.* Curtis also contributed teleplays to non-Western series like *Dr. Kildare, Ben Ca-*

*sey* and *Four Star Theater.* He lives on a ranch in Big Sur, California, with his wife, LaVon. In recent years Jack Curtis published numerous books of poetry, wrote *Christmas in Calico* (1996) that was made into a television movie, and numerous Western novels, including *Lie, Eliza, Lie* (2002), *Pepper Tree Rider* (1994) and *No Mercy* (1995).

We hope you have enjoyed this Large Print book. Other Thorndike, Wheeler, Kennebec, and Chivers Press Large Print books are available at your library or directly from the publishers.

For information about current and upcoming titles, please call or write, without obligation, to:

Publisher
Thorndike Press
295 Kennedy Memorial Drive
Waterville, ME 04901
Tel. (800) 223-1244

or visit our Web site at:

http://gale.cengage.com/thorndike

OR

Chivers Large Print
published by BBC Audiobooks Ltd
St James House, The Square
Lower Bristol Road
Bath BA2 3SB
England
Tel. +44(0) 800 136919
email: bbcaudiobooks@bbc.co.uk
www.bbcaudiobooks.co.uk

All our Large Print titles are designed for easy reading, and all our books are made to last.